Dark Betrayal

A Famiglia Novel #2

A.J. DANIELS

Dark Betrayal

A Famiglia Novel (book 2)

Copyright © 2018 by A.J. Daniels

Cover Design and Formatting: ©Just Write. Creations

Edited by: Hydra Productions

ISBN: 978-0-9958409-6-6

She was a savage
a fucking brute
Unafraid to fight for what she wanted
Brave enough to go to war for what she deserved.

R.h. Sin

She became dangerous to them when she no longer needed or cared
for their approval.

JMStorm

Dedication

To Neil (my dad), Eddie (grandpa), and Nora (granny), You may be gone but you'll never be forgotten. Thank you for always encouraging me to never give up and to pursue whatever it is that makes me happy.

Acknowledgements

To my hubby, thank you for being patient with me and taking on the majority of the household stuff when I was on a deadline. Thank you for bringing me wine and chocolate when the stress got too much. Thank you for being my rock. I love you to infinity and beyond, babe, and I can't imagine doing life without you.

My mom and brother, thank you for always encouraging me to pursue my writing, even when I was younger and had my nose stuck in a book or a pen and paper in hand. I love you and can't wait to see you at Christmas.

Laura, Andy, Sarah, Megan, Katrina, and Jeana, I'm incredibly blessed to have a group of friends who support and encourage me. Seriously, you guys make me cry every time you purchase a book or talk me up to other people. I love you. Thank you.

Sheila, my second mommy. Thank you for being there for me and treating me like a daughter when I had no family out west. I still can't believe my debut book traveled around the world haha.

Jo-Anna, thank you so much for another amazing cover and teasers. I can't wait to finally meet you in Vancouver and hug you. Thank you for all your support and encouragement.

Victoria, our random early morning messages give me life. Some days it's exactly what I need to make it through another day of writing and adulting. Thank you for your encouraging messages and your love of my mafia men, especially The Boss. Hawk is mine though, I put it in a book therefore, it's official haha.

Raven and Hydra Productions, thank you for jumping in when I needed an editor. I look forward to working with you in the future.

To my Beta and ARC readers, I value your opinions so much. I wouldn't be able to do what I do without you. Thank you for telling me what I *need* to hear, even if it's not always what I *want* to hear. Thank you for making me dig deeper. Your love and demand of these characters is what keeps me going.

Thank you to all the bloggers and reviewers. I hope you enjoyed Alessandro and Jessika's story as much as I enjoyed writing them.

And last but definitely not least, thank you to you, the readers. There is no doubt that without you I would not be able to do this. You guys demanded Alessandro and he's here, and I promise Antonio is coming haha. I can't say thank you enough, but THANK YOU.

Make sure to check the back for sneak peeks of the next book in the Famiglia series.

Blurb

What happens when you have to choose between loyalty to your family and loyalty to your heart?

JESSIKA

I begged, pleaded with them to not make me do it. To spare his life. It was the only thing I ever asked of them and instead of granting me my sole wish, they gave me an ultimatum.
Him or me.
If I couldn't choose, we would both die.

Could I sacrifice the man who saved me to save myself?

ALESSANDRO

She thinks I don't know the real reason for her seeking me out after two years. But I know. I've been watching her closely, anticipating the day she'll make contact. What I hadn't anticipated was my body's reaction to her when she stumbled into my apartment. But hell, as long as she's playing the game, I will too. I'll have her as much and in as many ways as I can get her until the time comes when the decision will have to be made; me or her.
Together we'll destroy each other.

Could I walk away from the girl with the emerald eyes?

Prologue

A **SLOW GRIN** tugs at the corners of her lips, the tip of the blade gleaming in the small beam of light right before piercing through skin like it was nothing. There is something about the sight of blood gushing from a throat wound followed by the gurgling sound that sends shivers down her spine.

The Bratva will be pleased with this latest kill. After all, this is what she was made for. They stole her innocence, broke her down into nothing so that they could rebuild and mold her into a machine. A black widow, if you will.

Wiping off the excess blood on the dead man's clothing, she re-holsters the knife in the sheath hidden inside the pocket of her leather jacket and zips up after tossing the black gloves.

The street is crowded with people on their way to their usual Friday night activities, no one the wiser about the monster hiding among them. It's not until she strips of her clothes and steps under the hot stream of water that she crumbles under the weight of it all. Sliding down the wet tile and bringing her knees to her chest, she allows the tears to mix with the steady stream of water from the shower head.

Another life lost. Another life was unnecessarily taken by her hand. One more and then she would be free.

They promised.

Chapter 1

"**DEEP BREATHS, JESS.** In. Out. In. Out. He's just a man," I tell myself. "Just a normal person. Nothing to be afraid of."

I groan, resting my forehead against the painted wood of the apartment door I'm currently standing in front of like a stalker.

Why I decided to try and find him, I have no idea. Morbid curiosity maybe? Fuck if I know. I did owe him a thank you for rescuing me from that hell, though, but that doesn't explain how I tracked down his name... and his number... and his address two years after the fact.

Well... it actually did. Klara and I talked a lot while we were held at the hospital. We bonded over the darkest time in both our lives and have been in contact ever since. I may or may not have let slip while we were leaving the hospital that I wanted to thank the man who had saved me, and she hadn't hesitated to give me his name and a number I could reach him at. I had the feeling, though, that she wasn't supposed to give me that information, but did anyway. She did not, however, give me his address. No, that I tracked down all by myself.

Yup, that's me. Jessika Tomlinson, stalker extraordinaire. To be fair, you can find anyone's address with a name and phone number. So, what did she expect? Probably not that I would show up on his doorstep, that was for damn sure.

I'm such an idiot. He's totally going to call the cops on me.

Just as I'm about to lift my forehead and turn around, having successfully talked myself out of this stupid plan, the door swings open, causing me to lose my footing and stumble forward into a very hard, very tall body. He grunts, catching me under my arms and standing me up, his hands never leaving my body until he's sure I'm steady on my feet.

"Sorry. I'm sorry. I was just-"

"Leaning against my door," he finishes for me.

"No," I cross my arms over my chest in a defiant manner. "well, maybe," I correct when one dark eyebrow raises in a try-again move.

Now that I'm standing in front of him I take a minute to take him in. He's tall. I mean massive, almost giant like. I'm five-six, and he easily towers over me by another foot. His hair is shaved down to his head, his grey eyes are striking against his tanned skin, and holy crap, talk about vein porn. The veins on his arms are fan-yourself-drool-worthy. His chest is broad, his stomach hard. I can see the ridges of his sculptured abs through the cotton of his muscle shirt when he crosses his arms.

"You about done looking your fill?"

Sweet Jesus, that voice. It's deep, seductive, and

coupled with his physique will probably be my undoing.

"Nope," I pop the 'p' continuing my eye fuck of the specimen in front of me. You'd think after what I went through in that make shift room of that cold, dark building that eye fucking a man, let alone thinking about all the things I'd like to do to him would be the last thing on my mind. But over the last two years, after realization sunk in that I wasn't living in that nightmare anymore, I've had a tough time thinking of anything other than the man who saved me from hell.

Strong hands grip my wrist, yanking me into the hard body my eyes were just taking in. "Did you come here to dance with the devil, Jessika?"

My breath hitches as I stare up into colorless eyes. "How did you know my name?"

"After two years, I know more than just your name, sweetheart."

"You've been stalking me?"

His other hand moves down to the dip in my lower back applying just enough pressure to bring me closer to his body. "Like you've been stalking me?"

"I came to say thank you."

Two years ago, Alessandro and Braxton De Luca, along with some of Braxton's other men, saved me from a rundown warehouse where I was kept chained to a dirty mattress as one man after another used me. Two years ago, this man saved my life and I never had a chance to thank him... until now.

He smirks, dipping his head and brushing his lips along my jaw turning my knees to jello, and if he wasn't holding me up, I'm certain I would've melted into a pool of need at his feet. "Haven't thanked me yet but if eye fucking me from across the room is your way of saying thank you, I'm going to need a lot more than that." His tongue licks up my jaw, his teeth nipping at my ear lobe causing me to shiver.

I swallow hard, my panties already growing damp. "Thank you."

"For what?" His breath is warm against my skin.

His lips hover just above mine, and I have to fight back a moan. "For saving me."

Abruptly he pulls away, taking those lips and the heat of his body with him as he takes several steps backward. I have to stop myself when I realize I'm seconds away from pouting and demanding he continues what he started. I watch him gather his wallet, keys, and holster a handgun before throwing on a leather jacket.

"Got somewhere to be, babe."

I follow him out, thinking we can continue a conversation as we both head downstairs, but as soon as he locks the apartment door behind us, he turns in the opposite direction and stalks off toward the stairs so fast that it leaves my head spinning. By the time I recover enough to follow him, he's gone.

***

ALESSANDRO

I needed to get out of there and fast because as soon as I saw her, got my hands, on her I wanted to claim her. Fuck, I wasn't ready for her to find me. I wasn't prepared for the tornado that is Jessika Tomlinson, but ready or not, she was here. And now that I've had my hands on her again I don't plan on letting go this time.

Prepare yourself, Jess. You're about to tango with the devil's second-in-command.

***

JESSIKA

Have you made contact?

I frown at the text as I get on the elevator and hit the button for the lobby, debating on how much to tell him. For the millionth time in the last two years, I wish I could disappear. Go anywhere, do anything, be anyone other than who I am.

I wish for a normal life. A life where nobody knows me, where I can leave my family -if you can even call them that- behind and make new ones in new friends. A life I could spend holed up in some cabin in the woods somewhere with only the sounds of nature to keep me company. Contradicting, isn't it? Wanting to make new friends but wanting to be so isolated that the only company I have are the sounds of birds and woodland creatures. What can I say, I'm a complicated one. Or not so much.

The things I want, the things I dream about aren't so different to anybody else's, really. I'm sure a lot of people wish they weren't born into the family they were. Forced to lead the life they were. Forced to lie and steal and cheat and destroy.

I always thought God must've had a sense of humor when he put me with the family he did. How else could I explain turning out to be the exact opposite of every one of my family members? I don't fit in with these people, never have and never will. Despite their attempts. Their attempts which included finally using the address I found all those years ago. I would've eventually tracked him down and thanked him. That part wasn't a lie. I just wasn't ready for that day to be today, but they were. And it was either them or me paying him a visit. I couldn't allow them to get their hands on Alessandro.

No. Nobody home.

I know this looks bad. After saying I hated lying, to then turn around and lie to my family, but was it still a lie if it kept the person safe? Was it still a lie if it offered protection, even though brief?

Make contact soon or sending someone else.

Yeah, fuck that shit. By 'someone else' I know that means my sister. I was not going to get her grimy hands on Alessandro. Not if I had anything to do with it.

Working on it.

I turn off the mobile device as I step off the curb and hurry across the street to the whited-out jeep. I breathe a little easier as my body sags against the black leather of the seats and the comforting aroma of the air freshener hits my nose. Mochadoodle.

Now, if only I could turn off my body's reaction to the giant of a man.

Chapter 2

ALESSANDRO

GREEN EYES FLASH in my mind's eye, and I curse as I push open the door to Braxton's home office, stopping when I get an eye full of Klara straddling him in the leather chair. I can't help the smirk that pulls at a corner of my mouth when her head snaps around at my entrance, her wild eyes locking on mine.

Then it dies at the memory of Jessika's skin under my palm when she stumbled through my door this morning. I'm glad Braxton finally got his happy, but seeing them together is making me itch to go after the woman who unwantedly managed to wiggle her way into my head. It was a rescue mission two years ago, and that's all it could ever be.

"Alex," Klara says, heat coloring her cheeks as she makes her way past me, closing the door behind her.

Braxton clears his throat, readjusting himself in his seat before moving closer and resting his elbows on the desk separating us. "Wasn't expecting you til later."

"Got an early start." I take up the seat across from him, a hand buried in the pocket of my coat, my thumb absently flicking the zippo lighter open and close. Open and close. Emerald eyes.

I need a smoke.

"The fuck's your problem, Alessandro? You're making me antsy."

I stop fidgeting, forcing my body to still. I don't fidget, ever. This girl is getting to me more than I'd fucking like.

"Got an unwanted visitor this morning." My lips move before I command them to.

"Oh?" Braxton sits back in his seat, an ankle crossing over a knee.

I rake a hand over my bald head, avoiding eye contact with the man who's been my best friend since we were in school. The man I've killed for. The man I'd die for. "That girl from the warehouse two years ago. The one next to Klara..."

I can't bring myself to continue. I've seen a lot of shit in my life, but that was by far the worst of it. The images that haunt me at night would be enough to bring any grown man to their knees. Braxton's cousin, Dante, was responsible for Klara's kidnapping two years ago. With the help of Klara's friend and a traitor within the Famiglia, they took Klara from her apartment in the middle of the night. When we finally tracked them down, Dante had broken her in more ways than one, but it wasn't just her. There were twenty other girls, most under the age of eighteen, being held against their will. We got them all out of there, and Braxton paid for their care and has continued to pay for any therapies the girls have needed. As for Rick, Gio, and Dante, they all got what they had coming to them.

"The one you carried out to the ambulance." It wasn't a question. His thumb runs over his mouth as he studies me and my reaction to the girl. "What did she want?"

Open and close. Open and close.

"To thank me for saving her."

Braxton nods, a quiet hum in his throat. "Did you fuck her, Alessandro?"

"No." My teeth hurt from the pressure I'm putting on them by clenching my jaw shut. I want to tell him to fuck off, but that'll cause an inquisition.

"But you want to?"

"Jesus Christ, Boss. She can't be much older than eighteen. I have no intention of touching her with a ten-foot pole."

"Twenty-two."

Fuck me. I didn't need to know her actual age. It doesn't change a damn thing. I'm still fifteen years older than her.

"I'm not fucking touching her," I growl leaning my elbows on my knees, flicking the lighter in the open now.

"Nobody said anything about touching her." Braxton chuckles and if he wasn't my Don and best friend, he would be wearing my blade. "Here," he says, tossing a file in front of me. "Take the new guy and go collect my money."

"You want me to take fresh blood on a collection call?"

He shrugs, amusement dancing across his face. "Let him learn from the best. Break him in."

I sigh, scrubbing a hand down my face but take the file and move to the door.

"Oh, and Alessandro, don't fucking kill this one."

"No promises, Boss," I smirk.

***

I watch from the shadows as the new guy threatens to break the fingers of the associate who thinks he can play the Famiglia. So far, he's doing good. The new kid, not the associate. I'd be surprised if he doesn't start begging for his life soon. I'm still not sure why Braxton sent me along, looks like he has everything handled.

Green eyes framed by long, black lashes fight their way through to the forefront of my thoughts. Then, my hands are back on that tight, tanned body, long midnight hair cascading down her back. My cock twitches behind the zipper of my jeans, forcing me to change my stance so I don't embarrass myself.

My mouth salivates at the thought of her writhing beneath me, screaming my name as she comes undone. In my head, her lips wrap around my cock, fingers gripping her head as I fuck her mouth. Her tongue swirls around the head of my cock.

My fists clench at my side. This is not the time to think of the girl. Forcing myself to pay attention to the scene in front of me, I notice the man in the chair is barely breathing, the new kid still delivering one solid punch after another. It's obvious he's not going to admit his transgressions, and I've about had enough of this.

Pulling the gun from the waistband of my jeans, I aim and have a split second when the new kid rears back again to pull the trigger. A bullseye between the fucker's eyes. The fresh blood calming me, albeit momentarily.

"What the fuck, Alessandro? He was about to talk!"

"He was already as good as dead." I re-holster the gun and push open the basement door, taking the stairs two at a time until I can smell fresh air again. I'm going to catch shit from Braxton for killing the snitch, but I couldn't give a shit right now. Right now, I just need a drink or two and a welcoming pussy.

Chapter 3

THE BAR IS packed by the time Stefan and I walk through the doors, but I spot her instantly sitting by herself at the bar, nursing a beer. Her dark hair is pulled up into a bun atop her head, showcasing her delicate neck. The arm of her shirt falls to reveal a smooth, tan shoulder and just enough hint of the top of a breast to elicit a growl from my chest.

She hasn't noticed me yet so I take the time to study her from across the packed room as Stefan and I take our usual seats in the booth at the back when the waitress places two cold beers in front of us. Her shoulders are hunched, her head down, eyes focused on fingers toying with the corner of the label on the bottle. Despite the fuck-off vibe she's giving, she's still garnering lots of attention from the male patrons. Male patrons that I won't hesitate to put down if any of them so much as looks at her wrong. I make my way through the crowd, feeling the need to stake my claim in the crowded bar.

My lips curl into a smirk when she stills against my chest. I lean forward, placing my hands on the bar on either side of her, caging her in. My already hard cock twitches when she sucks in a breath as my lips lightly skim up the curve of her neck, causing goosebumps to appear in their wake.

"Baby, if you were that sexually frustrated you should've said something earlier." I nip at her ear.

"I have no idea what you're talking about." Her chest heaves with the slight pant she's trying to hide.

I press in closer to her, making sure she can feel me hard behind my zipper. "You're picking at the label on your beer," I say by way of explanation.

"So?" She relaxes into me, her lips falling slightly open when I kiss a spot beneath her ear.

"You're telling me that if I dip my fingers under your panties I won't find you wet and hot for me? You want my cock, baby?"

Her back straightens, and she tries to put as much space between us as she can with me bent over her. "Not interested. Sorry." She gulps down the rest of her beer, signaling the bartender for a new one and avoiding all eye contact with me.

That's okay. I'll give her, her space now, but at the end of the night, she will be wrapped around me, my cock buried to the hilt inside her.

***

JESSIKA

Fuck. Fuck. Fuck.

I wasn't expecting him to walk into the same bar I've been sitting in for most of the evening. I was not prepared to deal with him tonight, hence the moment of weakness when I allowed myself to lean into him, touching him without actually touching him.

God, he was right. I was sexually frustrated. I wanted him. I wanted him with a need I never knew existed until I saw him earlier today. I can't mix business with pleasure, though. Or can I?

Nope, allowing him to get close will only spell disaster. So why am I disappointed when he eventually moves away, choosing to take a seat on the other side of the bar. Hiding in the shadows, the overhead lights of the bar glint off the silver of the lighter he's flicking open and close.

You want my cock, baby?

I did. I do.

"What's a pretty girl like you doing drinking in a bar by herself?"

I glance out the corner of my eye. This guy's not nearly as tall as Alessandro, and he's not bad looking either. Blond hair, blue eyes, a swimmer's body encased in an expensive suit, flashy gold watch on his left wrist. I can tell by his glassy eyes and wine flavored breath that he's been here since leaving the office hours ago. Maybe a quick bathroom fuck with Mr. tries-too-hard is exactly what I need to get Hulk out of my head.

"Well, I'm not alone now though, am I?" I say in my best sultry voice.

Shock flashes in his eyes before it's quickly replaced by lust, skimming down to check out my chest. "Buy you a drink?"

On a normal night, it would piss me off that his eyes have remained glued to my chest as he asks me the question, but tonight, I couldn't care less. I'm about to answer him when I feel a hard chest press into my back, strong arms wrapping around my waist.

"Take a hike," Alessandro says from behind me.

Blondie moves to tell Alessandro to fuck off without taking his eyes off me, but when he lifts his eyes away from my chest and takes in the hulking monster at my back, he visibly stiffens, his Adam's apple bopping with each hard swallow.

Pussy.

His fingers tighten around the wine glass in his hand, and then he scurries away. Eh, he probably wouldn't have been worth it anyway. The guy drank wine for heaven's sake. Not that there's anything wrong with a man enjoying a glass of wine or two on occasion. Ugh, who am I kidding? I want a man who enjoys the stronger shit, whiskey, bourbon...the good shit. If I wanted someone who drank wine, I would bat for my own team. Does that make me shallow? Probably. Did I care? Right now... not one bit. I'm pissed that Hulk scared off my only prospect of getting lucky tonight.

Unless...

Nope, not going to happen. I shut that thought down immediately and dead bolt it. I would sooner go home and dig out my vibrator than give in to my body's insistence on climbing the man standing behind me like a fucking tree.

"Was that really necessary?"

I shiver when his warm breath coasts over the nape of my neck. "I'm the only one who will be sampling this body of yours, Angel."

"So, what" I huff spinning in my chair to face him. "You're just going to chase off every guy in this bar who hits on me?"

Alessandro leans against the bar, crossing his massive arms over his chest, veins popping all down his forearms. I grip the wood bar a little harder, clenching my thighs together a little more.

"In this bar. In this city."

"You wouldn't dare."

Rough fingers grip my neck, forcing my head back.

17

Alessandro leans down until our lips are inches apart. "Try me. You were mine the second you stumbled into my apartment."

"I don't know what you're smoking, but I'm not yours."

I feel his chest rumble against my arm when he chuckles, then his teeth nip along my jaw before capturing my lower lip and tugging. It takes all the strength I have left today to not moan.

"Whatever you say, Angel," he whispers in my ear.

Cold air hits my neck when he removes his hand, and then he's turning and striding out the front door. I pay the bartender and don't bother finishing my now warm beer and go in search of one of the taxis that are usually parked along the street in front of the bar, trying like hell to not let my eyes search the parking lot for him.

Chapter 4

ALESSANDRO

I AM A fucking idiot.

I told myself I would stay far away from Jessika Tomlinson. I was not going to touch her with a ten-foot pole. She was too young. I knew she was far from innocent, though. She lived through and survived hell in that building two years ago. But her hell was nothing compared to what she would be facing if I allowed myself to take her to my bed.

It wasn't that I was afraid some stupid fuck would try and hurt her to get to me or Braxton like they had with Klara. No, I would burn them alive if they ever laid a finger on Jessika. It was that I didn't trust myself around her. I didn't trust that I wouldn't hurt her because I would. I would break her, snap her in half until she was just a shell of the person she is. I didn't trust that I could keep her safe from my own personal demons.

"Alessandro! Alessandro, what did you do?" I hear mother ask in the distance. Her voice sounds distant, though. Panicked. Why does she sound so distant?

I cock my head to the side, taking in the red, sticky liquid dripping from my small hands. It's still warm. So warm. The metallic smell oddly comforting.

No, this is wrong.

How did I get here? Where's father? Where's Johnny? We were supposed to go play in the treehouse after school. Where was my brother? Why hadn't he come to play?

"Vince!" my mother yells in the distance. "Vincent!" her voice still sounds so panicked.

"Don't worry, Ma," I try to soothe her. To let her know I'm okay.

I wasn't going to go play far. Just to the treehouse. But then my father's there, his dark eyes rounding in... shock, panic? He says something to mother, but I don't hear the words, I just keep staring at the red now staining my hands. Father begins to reach out to me, but stops suddenly and pulls back like I've hurt him. I'll never hurt him or mother.

Where's Johnny?

He's still not here. Father reaches down in front of me, then hauls himself to his feet. My eyes focus enough to see Johnny lying in his arms. A tree branch sticking out of his little body. I cock my head to the other side, looking from the tree branch to the red on my hands.

He didn't want to play.

I slam back the rest of the drink I poured as soon as I got home and head to my bedroom. Stripping down to nothing by the time I've reached the attached bathroom and turning the shower to the hottest it'll go. This had become part of my daily ritual ever since the day I realized what I had done. I couldn't get the water hot enough, couldn't scrub myself clean enough to forget the memory of my little brother's blood on my hands. Literally and figuratively.

My parents never looked at me the same after that day. They never mentioned my crime either, to the cops or each other. It was like that day had never happened. It was also the day I learned how to hide a body so that no one would find it, and if they eventually did, I learned how to make it impossible to identify. My father was my teacher, and he was fucking good at it. That day was the day that cemented my future.

I may be the Don's right-hand man, but there was also no one who could make a body disappear like I could. I think my parents were both relieved and scared shitless when Braxton befriended me my first day at a new school. Of course, they already knew the rumors and reputation his family held, but I think part of them also knew that there would come a day when they couldn't keep my demons satisfied any longer and were all too happy to pass that burden along to the De Lucas. Couldn't say I blamed them either. Who would want to carry the burden of having a murderer as a son? Not just that, but a son who had murdered their youngest boy. Their baby.

My parents' supervision slowly became nonexistent when Braxton, Antonio, and I became inseparable. I spent more time at Braxton's house with his family than with my own. Eventually, his dad told me to just move in, and I did. My father taught me how to hide bodies, Braxton's father taught me how to hide who I really was until the time came that I needed to embrace the fucked up part of myself. When he died, it was like losing my own father.

Blood may not have connected Braxton and me, but we were still family. Brothers. I will always have his back, and I know he has mine.

Grabbing a towel, I wrap it around my waist on my way into the bedroom and flip the switch turning on the lamp on the bedside table. My phone is staring up at me like a curse on top the polished wood. I could text her or call her just to hear her voice.

Just to hear her voice?

What the fuck?! I glance down at my semi-hard cock.

Nope, still have a dick.

My shoulders slump in mock relief. What is it with this woman and turning me into a pussy? I want to fuck hers, not become one myself.

Then why didn't you?

Sighing, I strip off the towel and climb beneath the clean sheets. I need to stop kidding myself. I am going to fuck Jessika Tomlinson. I just need to figure out how to do it without breaking her.

***

JESSIKA

"So, tell me again what the problem is, Jess, because I'm not understanding why you can't just climb him like a tree for one night?"

I groan, resting my forehead on my crossed arms as I sit bent over my best friend's dining room table. There isn't a problem, not really. The issue would be walking away after said one night. I don't think any woman has been able to walk away from Hulk after just one night. I mean, the man was built for pure dirty, rough, slam-you-up-against-the-wall sex. The kind of sex you walk away from with scratches, maybe a little bruising, and definitely a little sore. Which is fine with me. I don't want the sweet love-making most women want. I crave dirty, the rougher the better. The kind of sex I know Alessandro can give me.

"You know why, Mel."

"Ah, yes," she says, and I can hear her moving around her kitchen. "the little issue of your job."

"Wouldn't call it a job. It's not like I have a choice in the matter." Sitting up straighter in my seat, I grab the liquor Mel poured for me the minute my ass hit the chair in her kitchen, and gulp it down in one swallow.

"What would you call it, then?"

The hiss of the eggs hitting the hot pan echo around the room, and I don't even care that I'm day drinking at ten in the morning. Or would it be morning drinking? Fuck it, it's drinking.

"Punishment," I spit out the word as I go about looking through her liquor cabinet until I spot my prize.

"You could've said no. You know, put your foot down. Stand your ground and all that bullshit."

"And end up the one being buried six-feet under? No thanks." I pour a couple fingers of the liquid and gulp it back.

She sighs, turning the stove down before turning to face me. Her hands on her hips. "So, then, what's your plan, Jess?"

Pour. Gulp.

"I don't have one currently."

Pour. Gulp.

"Except for drink my expensive liquor, apparently." She shoots me a glare.

"Hey." I shrug. "It's either this or deal with the parentals." At this point, it would make more sense to drink straight from the bottle, but I'm still a fucking lady. "I'd much rather day drink, thank you very much."

"You're not going to find the answers at the bottom of that bottle, Jess."

She's right. I know this. Nothing good ever comes from trying to lose oneself to the bottom of a bottle of bourbon. *Fuck, that shit goes down smooth, though.* But hey, one could try.

I'm not an alcoholic. In fact, I barely drink, but between my father and Alessandro, it's either drink or fuck, and right now I can't do the latter.

"I should go," I say, placing my glass in the sink. "Have to sober up before doing a job tonight."

"You're not driving anywhere. Take the guest room."

A glance over my shoulder confirms that the deep voice belongs to Mel's new husband and a royal pain in my ass. Okay, that's not fair. Corey is a great guy, and he treats my best friend like a damn queen. But lately he's been doing this whole protective-big-brother thing with me, and it's starting to grate on my nerves. I've never had anyone look out for me, never needed it, and I don't plan on ever needing nor wanting it. I look out for myself. Always have. Always will.

You were mine the second you stumbled into my apartment.

I shove the memory away. I'm not his. I don't belong to anybody. I'm pretty sure if Alessandro knew the real Jessika Tomlinson, he wouldn't be so quick to make good on his statement.

"I'm good, Cor."

"You're drunk at ten thirty in the morning, Jess. You're not good."

"I'm not drunk."

"Yeah? How much have you had to drink, then?"

"Three drinks." The minute the words leave my lips, I feel my body sway at the same time Corey morphs into two. Shit, okay, so maybe I drank a lot more than I thought. Fuck, what was wrong with me.

"That's what I thought."

How the hell did he make it over to me that fast?

Corey slips an arm under my shoulder, taking most of my weight on him, and helps me navigate their house to the guest room. I barely register Mel saying she'll check on me in a bit through my alcohol soaked brain.

Chapter 5

"COME ON, BABY. You know you want it."

I'm barely able to swallow down the bile rising up the back of my throat as the man in front of me snakes his hand around to grab my ass, pushing his hips into mine. He smells like cheap liquor and cigarettes, and even cheaper perfume. Courtesy of the hooker he was with before I caught up with him. Now, he is in my web, and he isn't slithering his way out of this one.

The snake had managed to slip his way through a few sticky situations, leaving nothing but hurt and destruction in his wake. Little did he know that his time was about to be up. And I… I was tasked with being his fucking grim reaper.

I want to gag when I feel his puny dick press against my thigh, but I manage to school my features and fight the reflex. Instead, tilting my head to the side, I give him the illusion of me offering more of my throat for him to explore with his mouth. I revel in the feel of the cold, smooth metal sliding down my shirt sleeve until my fingers are wrapping around the handle.

"Give it to me," I whisper in his ear seconds before

the blade pierces his side. I twist, the knife scraping against bone - right between the ribs, nice - then pull it out, watching the snake curl in on himself as he collapses on the cold, hard ground.

After wiping the blood off the blade on his pant leg, I pull out my phone, one of many I use for moments like these, and snap a picture.

It's done

Turning the phone off and throwing it in the dumpster, I leave the alleyway in the opposite direction I entered it and loop my way around the block and back to my SUV, the alley in my periphery as I unlock the vehicle. There are no sirens. No crowd gathered. He'll bleed out alone, in a dark alley hundreds of people pass on a daily basis, but he won't be discovered until a homeless person decides to take shelter against the dumpster from the elements.

Another life avenged.

Another death cementing my place in hell.

Chapter 6

JESSIKA

> Russo's. 7pm. Wear something nice.

The fuck?

> Who is this?

> Alessandro

> How did you get this number?

I immediately save his number in my phone wondering when he got a new number because the one I already had in my contacts is completely different than the one he's texting me from, and ignore the flip my heart just gave at seeing his name on the screen.

> 7pm, Angel. I'll pick you up.

I snort. Obviously, he doesn't know me very well if he thinks I'm just going to take orders from him of all people. There's only one person I take orders from, and after this next job, I'll be truly free.

Or what?

The three little dots appear, stop, and then disappear before my phone rings.

"Don't test me, Angel. I have no problems bending you over and slapping that ass of yours." His growl sounds through the speaker.

I bite back a moan. "Promises. Promises."

Shit, why does my voice sound all breathy and seductive like? I need to tell him no and end the call.

End the call, Jessika.

"It's not a promise, Jessika." Even if he hadn't said that word, the promise in his voice told me all it needed to. I could run from him, but Alessandro loves the chase, he thrives on it.

As soon as I hang up the phone with Alessandro, I send an SOS text to Mel and then go in search of the emergency stash of beer at the back of my fridge. Despite knowing how fucked up this is - I'm supposed to kill him not go out on a date with him - I find that I'm actually looking forward to seeing him again. I'm looking forward to our back and forth banter, but more than anything… I want to feel his hands on me again.

"What the hell is so important that it warranted an SOS text?" Mel's voice carries through the apartment before I see her, the front door slamming closed behind her.

I barely contain the giggle that's threatening its way up because the only thing I see walking around the corner and towards me is a pile of clothes and Mel's small arms awkwardly wrapped around them. I barely see the top of her head over the monstrosity. I don't know whether to be amused or impressed that she made it up from the parking garage, through the building, and up the stairs with barely any vision. Oh, and managed to open my front door.

Ignoring her question, I move towards her and help by grabbing a few of the clothes on the top. Enough that her face becomes visible.

"Did you bring it?" I ask, looking through the dresses in my hand before discarding them on the kitchen island and going back through the pile for more.

Mel grunts, situating the rest of the clothes onto one of my arms so that she can reach down to her side and lift her purse that is overflowing with various makeup products.

"Now, are you going to tell me what all this is about?"

I turn my back on her and examine the black dress I just picked up from the pile. It's short, will probably hit about mid-thigh on me when it's on, and by the lack of stretch in the material, I'm guessing it's tight as fuck.

Perfect.

"I have a date with Alessandro," I throw over my shoulder at Mel and make my way to the bathroom to start the bath.

"You what?" Mel chokes, entering the bathroom behind me.

"It's not a big deal," I say, getting undressed.

I have no shame. Mel has been my best friend for as long as I can remember. She's the one who helped me to and from the bathroom when I had my appendix removed in high school because my family couldn't be bothered. If it weren't for her, I would've either been lying in my own filth until the stitches had healed enough, or I would've ripped them trying to do everything myself. She's the one who had to help me shower after another surgery when I could barely lift my arms enough to bathe myself. She's seen it all.

"Plus," I start, leaning my head back against the tub. "Weren't you the one who told me I should climb him like a tree at least once?"

"Since when do you listen to me?" she huffs, her hands flying to her hips.

"Since always," I grin.

"You're full of shit." She opens the cabinet, pulling out a clean towel and placing it on the towel rack so that I don't have to reach very far to grab it once I get out.

Best friends. Got to love them.

"You love me."

With an "mph" Mel closes the bathroom door behind her, leaving me in all my solitude which has been known to be a bad thing. I shouldn't be left alone, ever. Being left alone means everything running around in my brain has a chance to take purchase, which means I start obsessing. Like, what if the family doesn't let me bow out after this next job? What if I'm stuck in their clutches for the rest of my life? If circumstances were different and they allowed me to come into the family business when I was good and ready, then maybe I wouldn't feel so... betrayed? Stuck?

But they didn't. They kidnapped me, gave me to someone else who they paid to break me down. And then when that didn't pan out, they locked me away until I agreed to do their dirty work. To be clear, it's not the murders that I'm against. No, those sick fucks had it coming. It was the fact that the family thought they owned me. I jumped when they said. I lived where they said. I wasn't supposed to have friends because they forbid it. Mel being the exception, and the only reason I was allowed to see Mel was because of who her husband was.

Corey Jasvins was the most sought after lawyer for the organized crime families in the city. He also just so happened to be one of four partners at the firm. One of the other partners, Mason James, was the other most sought after lawyer for organized crime, except he belonged solely to Braxton De Luca. Nobody went near Mason who wasn't a member of *The Famiglia*. Which made him not only the second most sought after lawyer, but also the most hated lawyer in the city.

My family wasn't interested in Mason James, though. They wanted Corey in their corner, and if allowing me to cozy up to his wife would help them get him, then they were all for it. Little did they know that Corey wasn't interested in signing my family on as clients, he as much as told me that himself the first day we met. I was fine with it. I just wanted to hang onto Mel's friendship a little longer because as soon as the family found out that Jasvins would turn them down, I could kiss my only friend goodbye.

***

"For the love of God, Jessika, stop fussing." Mel grabs my arms and pins them to my sides, preventing me from continuing my cycle of pacing, running my hands down the dress, chewing on the corner of my thumb, and repeat.

Why the fuck was I so nervous? He was just a guy. The feeling of déjà vu hits, and I'm instantly reminded of standing outside his apartment door and having this exact same conversation with myself. Alessandro Ferrara is nothing special.

Yeah, keep telling yourself that.

"I look like an emo kid," I whine to my best friend.

I don't. I look hot in the fitted black dress, black pumps, and my dark hair straightened down my back. My makeup is simple with the emphasis on my full lips. But I'm stalling. Alessandro texted a few minutes ago saying that he was on his way and to be ready.

"You do not," Mel admonishes.

"You're right." I turn to the side, eyeing myself in the mirror. My body was toned and tight thanks to the copious amounts of training I was forced to endure starting when I was a teenager, and countless hours I spent in the gym maintaining it. "I look fucking hot," I tell my best friend, and she snorts.

"Alright, I'm out. Don't do anything I wouldn't do," she says, gathering the last of the makeup items and discarded dresses.

"Which is everything…"

Mel sighs, reaching for the door. "Just try to stay out of trouble. I don't want to have to explain to Corey why he needs to go bail your ass out at two in the morning."

Did I mention that Mel knows exactly who I am, who my family is, and what we do? It's part of the reason why I love her. She doesn't understand the reasoning behind why I do what I do, but she doesn't judge me. It probably has a lot to do with who her husband is and his client base. Mel's been good at keeping me focused lately too. She knows that I'm working on getting out, and when shit gets hard and all I want to do is throw in the towel, she reminds me of what I have to lose by staying in the game and everything I have to gain by being free.

Less than two minutes after Mel leaves my apartment there's a knock on the door. I'm both dreading and looking forward to opening it. I feel like a child whose parents are constantly telling them to not play with their food before they eat it. Except, I already know I'm not going to listen. I'm going to play with Alessandro til my heart's content, and then I'll devour him.

Chapter 7

"**T**HIS IS NICE."

Alessandro moves to pull out my chair for me when the waiter leads us to a table in a secluded area of the upscale Italian restaurant. The interior reminds me of one of the many restaurants I visited during my stay in Milan. Exposed wood beams run the length of the tall ceiling and down the wall. Vases with fresh flowers sit atop a pristine white table cloth on every table. Heavenly smells waft out from the kitchen, and I inhale deeply, fleetingly taken back to Italy and my too brief of a trip.

"They serve the most authentic Italian in the city," Alessandro states, lowering himself down in the seat directly across from me.

I'm momentarily disappointed that he chose to sit across the table and not next to me. I had plans on slowly seducing him through the night until his control snapped and he either dragged me out to his SUV or fucked me on the table in front of the whole restaurant. I didn't care.

When our waiter hands us each a menu I realize that Alessandro wasn't kidding about it being authentic.

Even the menu is in Italian, and I have no idea what any of the items are. I breathe a sigh of relief when he smirks over at me like he senses my dilemma and then begins to order for both of us, handing the waiter the menus before turning his grey eyes back on me. Whoever said French was the language of love had no fucking clue what they were talking about. I could listen to Alessandro speak Italian all night long.

"What did you order me?"

He grins, "What us Italians are famous for."

I quirk an eyebrow, waiting him out. Eventually, he shrugs a shoulder leaning back in the chair, giving me an unobstructed view of his chest muscles as they move under the white dress shirt. "Pasta."

Our waiter comes back and places a side plate of what looks like olive oil with balsamic vinegar in the middle then places a bread basket filled with focaccia bread in the middle of the table. I watch, curiously, as Alessandro breaks off a piece of the bread and swirls it in the oil vinegar combination before bringing it to his mouth.

"That," he says after swallowing his bite. "is the perfect ratio. Try it."

I follow his lead and swirl the specialty bread in the mixture, moaning when the flavors hit my tongue. He's right. The spices in the bread, the olive oil, and the balsamic vinegar were the perfect ratio to make a mouth-watering appetizer. I need to find out what the dish was called so that I can make it myself at home, even though it looks easy enough to duplicate.

When I look back over at him, I'm surprised to find him watching me so intently. His steal eyes focus on my lips. Lips that slowly tug up into a small grin as my tongue darts out to lick a split drop of balsamic vinegar from my finger.

I don't miss the way his nose flares and his fist clenches from where it's resting on the table in front of him. It lends to fueling my motivation to do what I'm about to do next.

Leaning back in my seat, I kick off a heel and bring my foot up to rest against the bulge in his pants. The table cloth covers the table and is long enough that if someone were to look over, they wouldn't be able to tell what I was doing to him.

"So, Alessandro, do you bring all the ladies here?"

His dick twitches against my foot as I slowly rub it up and down his growing length. *Come on, Alessandro, break.*

He braces both elbows on the table. His biceps are visibly flexing from his restraint. "I don't bring anyone here."

His statement throws me off, and I pause in my ministrations for a split second before shaking it off and refusing to analyze it any further. Alessandro grips my ankle when I apply a little more pressure against his bulge. His grey eyes turn dark with lust and a promise that I could be paying for this later.

He only releases my ankle when the waiter arrives with our food, and I straighten in my seat, forcing both my feet to stay firmly planted on the ground... for now.

"Tell me about yourself," I hedge, biting back a moan as the incredible rose sauce and perfectly cooked noodles assault my senses.

Alessandro grins. "They make the pasta fresh in house every day." He spears his fork through a shrimp covered in white sauce and pops it in his mouth chewing and swallowing his bite before answering my question. "Nothing to tell, Angel."

"Now that I don't believe. Where'd you grow up? Are you close with your parents? Any siblings?" I know all the answers to these questions, courtesy of my father, but I'm curious to see what *his* answers are. After all, there are always two sides to every story, and I'm particularly interested in what really happened to his brother. There are no records for his brother after childhood. No hospital records, no school records passed the age of three when he was in daycare. Nothing. It was like Johnny Ferrara existed one day and didn't the next.

"Italy. No, and I'm an only child." His response is clipped, leaving no room for discussion. His eyes are cold when they hold mine. He wants me to drop the subject, and I'm torn.

Part of me – the part that has business to take care of – wants to know all his secrets so that I can use it to somehow justify this job. I want him to unknowingly confirm that my father is right in wanting him eliminated. That he's not on the list just because of his association with Braxton De Luca. But another part of me is telling me to drop it. That it's really none of my business, and if Alessandro wants to tell me, he will. The angel and the devil are in a tug of war on my shoulder, but eventually, the angel wins, and I drop it… for now.

"I love Italy. I spent several days in Milano one summer. It wasn't nearly long enough, but I fell in love with the cobble stone streets, the wine, and the food. Everyone seemed so laid back too."

Alessandro finishes his dinner, taking his time chewing the last bite before he speaks. "Were you able to visit anywhere else?"

"No." I take a sip of wine and allow my gaze to

wonder around the restaurant again. "I always wanted to go back. Rome. Vienna. Tuscany. I used to want to see Italy in its entirety. Even the places that aren't usually visited by tourists."

"Used to?" he asks.

I try to school my features in a neutral expression when I look back over at him, but a small, sad smile breaks loose. "Traveling just isn't in the cards right now," I say, hoping he'll change the subject now.

If I'm lucky, and my father kept his word, then maybe that dream is still possible. Maybe this time next month I'll be exploring Italy the way I've always wanted to. *Yeah, and maybe unicorns do exist.*

Ugh, enough of this. I agreed to this - whatever this is - for a reason and it was time to make it happen.

I slowly run my foot up Alessandro's leg until my heel is resisting against what I can only hope is an impressive package, and look up at him from under lowered lids. "Why don't we get out of here?"

I don't think I've seen anyone ask for and pay a bill at a restaurant as fast as Alessandro did. In less time than it should've taken us to get back to my apartment, he's pulling the SUV into the underground parking lot of my building.

Alessandro no sooner has the car in park and turned off, then he's reaching over and undoing my seat belt. Strong hands grip my hips, and I'm in the air and straddling him, my hands braced on a rock-solid chest while something else rock-hard digs into my thigh.

I can't hear anything other than my own heavy breathing as Alessandro skims his hands up my bare thighs, one hand gripping my ass and pulling me closer, the other snaking up to curl around my hair and tug my head back, exposing my throat to his wandering lips.

"You sure you want this, Angel? Once we cross this line, there's no going back." He nips along my jaw. My body feels like it's on fire. "Once my cock gets a taste of this pussy, I'm going to fuck you where I want when I want, and all you get to say is yes, sir."

I swallow hard. His dirty words are a direct line to my throbbing clit. "Yes, Sir."

"Good girl." He licks and nips my throat. "Now, take me out. Stroke me."

My fingers fumble with his belt, but I finally pull him free after what feels like fucking forever. He's warm and hard and smooth against my palm. A grunt fills the car when my hand tightens around the base, and I stroke his length. Up and down. Up. Down.

For as long as I can remember the thought of almost getting caught would ratchet up my need for more. Harder. Faster. Just more. And right now, with my aching core pressed against him and Alessandro moving my panties out of the way and sliding his fingers into my wet heat, the thought of being caught sets my body ablaze. I need him inside me, and nothing short of the world ending will stop me from getting what I want.

He must know what I want because his fingers slip out of me and curl under my thighs, lifting me up only high enough for him to position me, and then he's slamming home in one long, singular push.

Dear lord, I feel like I've just been impaled. Legit impaled.

Alessandro groans low in his throat, and then he starts moving, lifting me up and slamming me down while he rocks up into me. Pain and pleasure start mixing together until the only thing left is pure unadulterated pleasure.

I rock my hips more, meeting each of his thrusts

with one of my own. Alessandro pulls my head back more, causing my back to arch, my tits in his face, his cock hitting deeper with each of his upward thrusts.

I knew this Hulk of a man was made for fucking, but this... this was animalistic. There were no emotions, no promises of forever, no whispered words of love. It was lust. It was raw. It was a basic human need being satisfied. It was carnal, and it was dirty as fuck.

"You have a greedy pussy, Jessika. Fuck, I can feel it sucking me in. Every fucking inch of my dick. You're going to come for me, Angel," he grunts. "You're going to come so fucking hard around my dick, then I'm going to fuck this pretty throat, and you're going to swallow everything I give you."

Fuck me. His words. I've never had somebody talk dirty to me before and actually be good at it, but with every filthy word that leaves his mouth my body tightens. And when his thumb finds my clit and presses down, it's like detonating a bomb. I do exactly what he commanded, I come the hardest I've ever come in my fucking life.

Before I have a chance to come down from my post orgasmic high, Alessandro lifts me up from his lap and pushes me down until I'm kneeling on the floor of the SUV under the steering wheel. One giant hand wraps around the back of my head and forces my face down until my lips part around the head of his cock.

Alessandro fucks my mouth until my jaw aches, and I can barely breathe, tears sliding down my cheeks. With one more deep grunt, warm, salty liquid hits the back of my throat, and I swallow spurt after spurt of his cum until I've sucked him dry.

Chapter 8

"**H**ELLO, SISTER."

My body stiffens at the sound of the familiar voice despite not having heard it in years. Fuck, I really need to start screening the unknown calls. But then what would be the point? They'd just come up with more creative ways of finding me.

"What do you want, Amanda?" I ask, forgoing the coffee for something much, much stronger. Then I remember the long ass day ahead of me, so I pour the coffee anyway, but instead of my usual coffee creamer, I opt for Bailey's.

"Been getting pretty cozy with your mark, aren't you? Really, Jessika, in a parking lot?" she tsks, ice filling my veins with the realization of what she said.

"You're having me followed?!"

"*Dad* is having you followed," she corrects, the irritation clear in her voice. "He doesn't think you have what it takes to end this, and frankly, after seeing your little show, I have to agree with him."

Slamming my hand down on the granite countertop, I hiss into the phone, "Do not touch him, Amanda. I'm handling it."

"Then handle it, little sister. Although, I wouldn't mind taking that hulk of a man for my own spin before putting a bullet in his head." Her voice takes on an almost dream like quality, like she's picturing riding Alessandro herself.

The ice in my veins thaw, my blood now boiling with the thought of Amanda and Alessandro together.

"You fucked up with Braxton. What makes you think you can even get close enough to Alessandro?"

Our father sent Amanda to get cozy with the Italian Mafia Don. Her job was to seduce him, make him fall in love with her, and marry her. Thus, giving her access to every aspect of his life and giving our father the in he needed to get rid of Braxton and take over as the biggest, most respected crime family on the east coast. Amanda did everything right. She got the rock with the wedding only a week away, and then she fucked up. Braxton caught her sexing it up with his cousin, Dante, and ended the engagement. Amanda was pissed. Our father was even more pissed because it forced him to find another way into the De Luca family.

Then Braxton went and fell in love, and our father found a confidant in Giovanni, one of three people Braxton kept apprised of his every day dealings. Turns out Gio had his own revenge planned for Braxton, but still nobody knows exactly why Gio has it out for Braxton. However, I'm assuming that's not exactly true because I suspect my father does.

Dante and Gio's orders were simple. Kidnap the girl, make Braxton sweat and beg for her back, and then kill him when he was at his weakest. They both failed. Miserably. Both ended up dead at the hands of the Mafia Don. Now, I was our father's third and possible last option in bringing down Braxton.

Of course, I wasn't made aware of all this until after battling through my own personal hell and leaving that hospital to find my father lying in wait for me.

Daddy dearest thinks that since Braxton and Alessandro are practically brothers in every sense of the word while they may not share blood, Braxton will feel like he's losing his control when faced with Alessandro's murder. Maybe lose it enough that his reputation will take a nose dive and people will turn on him. My father plans on stepping in and *taking care* of Braxton. Effectively restoring balance to organized crime.

I would never tell my father this, but there is a flaw in his plan. I don't believe Braxton will lose his control. I think Braxton will do exactly what he did when Klara got kidnapped, but maybe worse. I believe Braxton will hunt down everyone he ever suspects in Alessandro's death until he finds the killer – me and by extension my father and the Bratva. Absentmindedly, I reach down and scratch the tattoo on my upper thigh.

"Oh, sweet, naïve, Jessika. I should be offended that you think so little of my skill. I just need to get him drunk enough that he believes I'm you," she giggles like it's the funniest thing in the world.

"Stay. Away. From. Him," I snarl each word. Family or not, I will not hesitate to put a bullet in her head if she even thinks about cutting my time with Alessandro short. I plan on using Hulk as much as I can before his time is up.

"Handle it, Jessika, or I won't have a choice."

With that, she ends the call. As soon as I hear the click, my phone goes sailing across the room before hitting the wall and falling to the wood flooring.

Three things become glaringly obvious to me at this

moment. One, I either need to pull up my big girl panties, close off my emotions, and take care of business. Two, I need to find something my father wants equally as bad as he wants Alessandro dead and hope that takes his attention away from the Italian Hulk. And three, I am way too attached to the man after one dinner and a quick fuck in his car.

Option one ensures my freedom from the reach of the family. Hopefully. Option two results in both our deaths. No matter how much I turn that scenario over and over in my head, I know deep down to my bones that the only thing my father will want more than Alessandro's blood is Braxton's. If Alessandro ever found out that I was the one who pulled the trigger on Braxton, *he'd* be the one to kill me, and I just wasn't down with that. I needed to find a way to get Alessandro to let down his guard around me enough for me to take care of business. Starting with another round of dirty fucking.

I refuse to even think about the third thing because Alessandro means nothing to me except for being someone who knows how to fuck me within an inch of my life.

As soon as I make sure that my phone screen isn't cracked and it's working fine, thanks to the kickass protective case, I shoot off a quick message, trying to fight the grin that threatens to pull at the corners of my lips.

He's just a means to satisfy an urge, Jessika. Nothing more.

My place. 20mins.

***

45

ALESSANDRO

My knuckles had barely left the painted wood of the apartment door before it's being ripped open. Jessika grabs hold of the front of my shirt and tugs me inside, pushing me up against the door once it's closed behind me and attacking my mouth with one hell of a kiss.

"Hello to you too, Angel," I manage to get out when we come up for air.

"No talking. More fucking," she breathes, already pushing my shirt up and off.

Her eyes ablaze with lust when she takes in the smattering of dark hair on my chest, and darken even more as she traces my happy trail down to where it disappears under the waistband of my jeans.

"Keep looking at me like that, Angel, and you won't be walking tomorrow," I growl.

Her tongue darts out to run along her bottom lip, and I swear she whimpers when she finally takes in the defined V of my pelvic muscles. The one that drives women crazy.

Jessika continues eye-fucking me while stripping off her tight tank top and sliding down her sleep shorts, leaving her standing completely naked except for a smile.

I swallow hard in an attempt to calm myself down because if I don't I'm not going to be able to hold back on her anymore, and I'll do more than just make sure she can't walk tomorrow.

"Run," I rasp out, fists clenching at my sides so that I don't reach out and grab her. "Run, Angel, because when I catch you, I'm not going to stop fucking you until I've had my fill."

I open my eyes and pin her with a stare that tells her

exactly what I have in mind once I catch her. Her pretty emerald eyes widen in shock before she takes off down the hallway, but I catch up to her in three easy strides. Jessika giggles when I spin her to face me and throw her over my shoulder in a fireman hold. Slapping her ass, I make my way down the hall and to her bedroom.

She bounces when I deposit her on the soft mattress and strip out of my jeans, pulling my socks and shoes off with them. I catch a brief glimpse of a tattoo on her outer thigh but then my attention snaps back to the gorgeous girl on her back in the middle of the bed, her legs spread wide for me. Her fingers already playing with her clit.

The shriek that leaves her throat when I pull her by her ankle closer to me makes me burn hotter. Pre-cum leaks from the tip of my dick. With her legs resting on my arms, I lean over her, practically folding her in half, my hand wrapping around her pretty throat, and she moans. She fucking moans, when I squeeze just a little tighter.

I could tell when she was playing with herself that she's already wet, so without missing a beat I slam home in one thrust. Jessika arches her back beneath me, taking me deeper until I'm buried to the hilt. I don't give her time to adjust before I start fucking her like both our lives depend on it.

"Ah, fuck! Harder. Please," she begs, her pussy tightening like a vise around my dick.

"Your wish is my command," I growl, removing my hand from her throat and biting down on her shoulder as my hips piston harder and faster, fucking her like she begged. "Fucking hell, Jess," I roar when she tightens around me, her body shuddering with her orgasm, and milks my cock until there's nothing left. I collapse beside her, trying to get my breathing under control.

"Hi." She turns to me and smiles after several minutes, her hand already finding its way back to my cock.

Chapter 9

JESSIKA

ALESSANDRO FUCKED ME until I could barely see straight, let alone think straight, which was great because it meant my brain stopped working long enough for me to get some decent sleep. I did manage to kick him out before I succumbed to the dreamless sleep that beckoned to me after the last time we used each other's bodies. I couldn't tell you what his reaction was to being kicked out because I was lights out as soon as the order left my lips. I'm not supposed to care anyways. I'm just using his body until I can devise a plan to end his life.

"Wake up, bitch! It's shopping day!" Mel hollers, closing the front door behind her. She stops short of entering the kitchen and wrinkles her nose. "It smells like sex in here." Her eyes round in realization, and if I could I would shrink further into my oversized hoodie to hide the heat creeping up my cheeks. "Holy shit, did you bump uglies with Hulk-man?"

I groan, "Bump uglies? Seriously, Mel?"

"What?" she shrugs like she really has no idea how ridiculous she sounded. I love my best friend, I do, but I just can't with her right now. But I know she's not going to let it go until I give her something.

"Yes, we fucked each other's brains out, and then I kicked him out. By the way, *bitch*? Who are you and what have you done to my best friend?"

"What? I call you a bitch all the time. It's our thing."

I snort. "It's never been our *thing*."

"Whatever," she sighs, rolling her eyes and not meeting my gaze.

It's then I get a good look at her. Something feels off. Sure, she looks fine, but something about the way she's acting today and her choice of words aren't sitting right with me. I get up to make her a coffee, adding extra Bailey's to her cup - I was planning on driving us today anyway – before making my way back to the bar stool and pulling out a seat for her.

"Tell me what's with the mood today, and don't say nothing, because I know it's something."

Mel huffs but takes the seat next to me, curling her hands around the coffee mug I put in front of her.

"You know Mason, Corey's partner at the law firm?"

I nod for her to continue, bringing my own cup up to take a sip.

"His wife just died from cancer last month. He seemed like he was handling it okay. The guy's wife died, and he still never missed a day at the office. He even started working more overtime. Until about a couple weeks ago. Corey got worried that he hadn't shown up at the office for several days, so he went over to Mason's house," she pauses taking a sip of her coffee. "It was bad, Jess. Cor said it looked like he hadn't showered in almost a week, and probably hadn't eaten in just as long. Cor managed to get Mason cleaned up, but he wasn't convinced that the guy would start taking care of himself again. He called me and we agreed that the best thing for Mase was if Corey brought him home to stay in our guest room so that we could make sure he at least ate daily. Until he was okay enough to take care of himself."

I sensed there was more that she needed to say so I kept quiet and give her time.

"One week, Jessika. I haven't had sex with my husband in one week. Seven days."

I cough and sputter on the mouthful of coffee I'm trying not to spit in my best friend's face. "What?" That was so not the direction I thought this conversation was going. Not at all.

"Don't get me wrong. I love Mason. I feel for him. They were high school sweethearts, and I can't imagine losing Corey. But between his own clients, taking on some of Mason's missed work load, and Mason living with us, I haven't seen my husband. I need to get laid, Jess. I'm a woman with needs."

I sit, staring at her, slack jawed. My mouth opening and closing like a guppy while I take in everything she just told me. And I realize if I were in her shoes I'd feel the same way. Hell, now that I've had a taste of Alessandro, I'm not sure if I could give that up. I immediately shake the thought away because nothing good could come from the train of thought. I'm going to have to give him up. End of story.

"Does Corey have a lock on his office door? Can anyone see in, even with the door closed?" I ask.

"Yes, to the lock. No to the other one. What's going on in that messed up head of yours?"

I think about it for a minute, finishing my coffee, and then grin as I place the mug gently on the counter before turning to my best friend. "Okay, here's the plan. We're going to go shopping like we planned.

We're going to get you some sexy lingerie. Something Corey can't ignore. Then, we're going to get your hair and makeup done, you're going to slip into something sexy sans panties, and then you're going to go visit him at the office. You're going to give him a little preview of what he can look forward to when he gets home. When he walks through the front door, you'll greet him in nothing but the lingerie and a pair of fuck me heels."

And that's what we did. I drove us to the mall then proceeded to drag Mel to every store until we found the perfect outfit and lingerie for her day of seduction. Mel started complaining about ten minutes in, but I could tell that she secretly loved it. What woman wouldn't love shopping for an outfit that could bring her man to his knees and cause him to beg?

I may or may not have picked up something for Hulk as well. Not that I would ever admit that it was for him. After all, every woman deserves to feel sexy in a stunning outfit and hot lingerie. So, the items I picked out were solely for me and me alone, and if he just so happened to catch a glimpse of them while he was ripping it off my body, then he does.

Mmhm, yup. All for me.

So, I have no idea why I took the picture I did as soon as I got home, showered and changed. Or why I found myself sending said picture to a certain male.

***

ALESSANDRO

"Holy shite," Stefan chokes out next to me. "Ow, what the fuck, Alex?" he says, a hand rubbing at the spot where I just hit him at the back of his head. I pin him with a glare, and he shuts the fuck up.

My anger has been off the charts today. I have enough tension coursing through my body to rival all other days. The tension in my body is coiled so tight, like a snake waiting to strike, anything could set me off, and I have no fucking clue why.

The job Braxton sent Stefan and I on went off without a hitch. The stupid fuck sang like a fat woman at the opera. I like when they tell me what I want to know without me having to get blood on my clothes. It's a bitch to get out, and I'm tired of buying new clothes. He made my job so much easier today so I should be riding the high that comes with knowing we're that much closer to closing this deal for Braxton and adding to his ever-growing fortune. Then why do I feel like shit's about to hit the fan and fuck up everything we've worked years to achieve.

I just need to fuck out this tension, and I know the perfect way to do it. My cock hardens, and a grin spreads across my face as I take another look at the picture that just came through in a text message. I admit my ego took a hit when she kicked me out of her apartment after I made her cum so hard she could barely speak. A beer and burger later, and I was over it. I've kicked out my share of women. Hell, it's not like I want anything more from Jessika than what her body could do for me.

And what a fucking body it is. Curves for days. The woman has enough meat on her bones that I don't have to worry about breaking her in half when I fuck her hard. Hips I can actually grab onto and an ass that bounces when I pound into her from behind. I groan low in my throat at memories from last night.

Fuck this. She wants to play. Well, game on, Angel.

"I'm out," I tell Antonio, slapping a hand on his

back as I make my way past him while Stefan snickers where I left him sitting.

"Brax is meeting with the lawyer tomorrow. He's going to want you with," Antonio says, catching my attention before I can push open the door.

"Thought Mase was still off," I say, turning back to Antonio.

"He is. Corey Jasvins is taking on some of his clients while Mase is out. Brax wants to meet with him. He's not so sure he can trust him with the man's Russian connections."

Mason James is the primary lawyer for the Famiglia. When shit goes down, Mason bails our asses out. He's also paid to make sure that we don't go down. Corey Jasvins is another partner at Mason's law firm. However, Corey has nothing to do with the Famiglia, but he is on some of the other families' payroll. Which makes me weary of this whole situation. I vowed to always have Braxton's back, and I always will.

"I'll be there." I nod at Antonio and then head out. I have some tension to fuck out, and I know just the girl to help.

***

JESSIKA

I was expecting the knock on my door, but it still made me jump. I momentarily consider pretending not to be home. The text was a spur of the moment thing. One I wish I can say that I regretted sending but deep down, I'm not. Not one bit. I wanted him to come over, and that text practically ensured that he would move heaven and hell to get here.

Alessandro's fist pauses mid-air when I pull open the

door. His eyes darken to an impossible black as he takes me in. Did I mention that I never bothered to change out of the new lingerie I bought?

An embarrassing squeak works its way past my lips when Alessandro rushes me. Picking me up by my thighs, and kicking the door closed behind him, he pins me to it. My legs wrap around his hips. He nips and sucks up my neck, while each hand grabs a handful of my tits.

"I can't wait to peel you out of this, but right now my dick misses you," he rasps against my neck. His thick fingers work their way under the lacy thong and finding me already soaked for him.

"Please, Alessandro." I'm not above begging for what my body so readily craves. I need him inside me. I need him to fuck me so hard that my brain shuts off. That I forget about my responsibilities. I need him to make it all go away. To make me forget who I am.

The sound of a belt being undone breaks through my running thoughts, seconds before he's pushing his way inside me. A sigh escapes me as he fills me.

Fuck yes.

Just like last night, Alessandro doesn't give me a chance to adjust to his size before he's slamming home. Harder. Faster. Relentless. Just the way I like it. I'm not a big fan of foreplay. I'm more interested in what comes after. Foreplay usually means there's some sort of emotion involved. An emotion that I can't afford to have. Not with Alessandro. Not ever.

"Your pussy's greedier than ever, Angel. Was this what you were hoping for when you sent that picture?" Alessandro growls in my ear, his one hand closing around my throat. Another thing I like about Alessandro, he wasn't afraid to get rough with me. He doesn't treat me like I am fragile. He takes what he wants, and I am all too willing to give it to him.

"Fuck yes," I groan, repeating my earlier thoughts.

My nails dig into his wide shoulders when his thrusts get harder. I'm so close I can feel it, almost reach out and touch it, but it's still a little out of my grasp. Alessandro leans up enough to rub my lips with his finger until I part them. He finger fucks my mouth until my jaw aches, then he's reaching down to part my ass cheeks, and the pad of one finger rubs against my puckered hole before pushing in. The burn is just what I needed to send me over the edge and I come... hard.

Alessandro continues his hard thrusts while his finger fucks my ass. Then, he comes with a roar, and I swear it's the sexist sound I've ever heard. Spurt after spurt of warm cum fills me until Alessandro leans his forehead against mine, spent.

It's not until I'm standing in the shower on shaky legs and reaching out for my body wash do I remember that his cum's running down my inner thighs and that we never used a condom.

"Well," I whisper to myself, "at least I can never get pregnant."

Alessandro joins me in the shower a minute later, effectively silencing most my racing thoughts until the only one left is how many times I can use this man tonight, and in how many positions. He didn't get to peel the new lingerie off me, but I have something else that he may like a little better. Something that he can rip off.

I have a feeling neither one of us is getting much sleep tonight. Totally fucking worth it.

Chapter 10

ALESSANDRO

"**WHO'S THE CHICK?**" Braxton asks as I round my car to meet him at the steps of the law firm.

"There's no chick." I stop in front him, adjusting my tie and jacket to keep my hands busy so that I don't ball them into fists and give myself away. The fact that I'm instantly defensive over Jessika says a fuck ton, but I'd be damned if I let Braxton know that. He may be my boss, but he's also my best friend, and he's guaranteed to give me shit over my not-relationship with Jess.

I'm not a one-woman man. Never have been. Never thought I would ever be. I like sex. As much as I can get, whenever I can get it. It's no secret in our circle that I've been known to often bring multiple people into my bed. Male. Female. Fuck if I care. As long as I'm getting laid my dick's happy. And he's been a very happy boy the last few nights.

"Spit that bullshit somewhere else, Alex. You forget I've known you since you were fifteen. Never known you to only have one person in your bed for this long. Who is she?" Braxton crosses his arms and leans against the side of his sports car like he has all the time in the world.

"Jessika Tomlinson."

"She the girl you carried to the ambulance from the building? The one being held next to Klara?"

I tip my chin in a slight nod, watching his every reaction. It's no secret that Braxton still blames himself for Klara being taken. I don't know why. The only thing the guy did wrong was fall in love. Everything that happened after that was just a bunch of dumb fucks who thought they had what it takes to take down the Famiglia. Even if one of them did just so happen to be his very own cousin.

If we're being all honest and sharing our feelings and shit, I don't think Braxton was wrong in falling in love. Having a partner for life who accepts you no matter what your fuck ups are, who will be there to welcome you home at two in the morning and with blood stains on your clothes, who will unconditionally stick by you through everything this life has to throw at you, that's what makes all the shit we deal with on a daily basis worth it - to know that at the end of the day we have that one person in our corner.

Braxton glances up and to the right of me, his eyes taking on a faraway look, one I don't like because it means he's remembering something... something that I'm not going to like, but instead of saying anything about it, he turns and heads for the front door of the law offices effectively ending our conversation.

Braxton's meeting with the temp lawyer goes smoothly. I have to admit that Corey Jasvins impressed me. He answered all of Braxton's questions and put his concerns to rest about his Russian connections. Apparently, he refuses to do business with them regardless of the boost it could do to his financial situation and early retirement. Jasvins said he wasn't comfortable in taking on the Russian crime family since the firm already represents the De Luca family, thanks to Mason James who is the one and only lawyer to take on organized crime in the law firm. Which shocked the fuck out of me. I thought both James and Jasvins were on organized crimes payroll. By Braxton's reaction or lack thereof, I'm guessing he already knew that.

Jasvins explains what happened with James' wife, and since the Famiglia doesn't have any pressing cases or being threatened with possible charges, Braxton agrees that giving Mason James some time off is the best thing for him and for us.

An hour later we leave the lawyer's office, but not before Braxton reminds Jasvins that if he even thinks about screwing over the Familgia there is no place he can hide that we will not find him.

"Go home, Alessandro," Braxton says, slapping a hand on my back as his driver opens the door to the backseat. "Take the weekend off. I'm taking Klara to Italy this weekend anyway. We'll see you at family dinner Sunday night," he says before getting in the car.

I don't bother arguing with him. Why look a gift horse in the mouth and all that shit? I hit the top of the car after closing his door and watch them drive away, but my mind is on Jessika and all the ways I can make her come in forty-eight hours.

The answer? A-whole-fucking-lot.

Jess and I have done a lot of fucking since the first time in my SUV, and if I plan on milking her body for every single last orgasm it can give, then I'm going to need some fuel. Heck, food can be an aphrodisiac too, and I plan on slowing things down tonight. Drawing out her pleasure, drive her to edge but not allow her to go over until she begs, and even then, I'll only let her come when I'm good and ready for her to come.

I watch the three dots appear only to disappear a moment later with no message. Her reply finally comes through when I'm already five minutes away from her place.

***

JESSIKA

"You're cooking?" I ask Alessandro when I let him in and he heads straight for the kitchen, arms laden with bags of groceries.

This is not good. Not good at all.

It's one thing to share a meal together at a restaurant, but it's something else entirely to cook for someone. Cooking for someone implies a level of intimacy. It implies a relationship of some sort, whether that relationship is family, friend, or romantic in nature. The fact that Alessandro was in my apartment prepared to cook for me… us means that this - whatever this is - means more to him than it should. Whether he wants to admit it or not.

I'm already starting to get attached to him in ways I cannot afford to. Hell, I bought lingerie with him in mind for fuck's sake! I wouldn't do that if this was still just some mutually beneficial fucking. I find myself looking forward to his sexts in the middle of the day. I look forward to him showing up at my door at night. And last night when he left I was disappointed because a part of me wanted him to tell me he was staying and fuck what I said.

I just violated my first rule. Never get attached to a mark.

"Figured it was time I show you what real fettuccine is supposed to taste like."

"What makes you think I don't already know what it's supposed to taste like?" I ask, opening us each a beer.

Alessandro snorts and gestures to the frozen dinner packages I forgot to take down to the dumpster. "I saw the same packages the last time I was here and you kicked me out."

"What?" I shrug, taking a sip of my beer. "I hate cooking and they're easy."

"And full of shit."

His response doesn't surprise me. After all, there's no way he got to look like the way he does by eating crap. My guess is that when Alessandro goes grocery shopping he only buys the cleanest ingredients, he never allows himself a cheat day, and he probably works out for hours every day. It wasn't a hard guess. It's what my life was like growing up. Father always wanted us in the best shape. When Amanda and I weren't in school, learning to fight, or learning to shoot we were in the gym. We didn't eat anything that didn't get his approval first. Hence my current attachment to alcohol, any and all food that's bad for me, including the giant chocolate bar in the fridge and the tub of ice cream hidden in my freezer. I was just making up for lost years.

After setting the table, I watch Alessandro work in

my kitchen like he was born to be there. I soon find myself mesmerized by the fluidity of his movements. Alessandro makes it all look effortless. His muscles pull and strain under the crisp dress shirt as he stirs the sauce in the pan while it thickens. The veins in his forearms popping while he chops parsley for the garnish.

I watch him carefully plate the pasta and sprinkle the garnish on top before picking up both plates and setting one down in front of me, but eating is the furthest thing from my mind. Well, eating food is the furthest thing from my mind.

My mouth waters at the memory of his taste. I can't wait to wrap my lips around his favorite appendage and watch as I bring him to the edge. Knowing that it's me that does that to him. It's me who makes him groan low in his throat. It's me who causes that deep growl to rumble through his chest. It's my body he worships like it holds the key to his happiness.

"Keep looking at me like that, Angel, and I'll be attempted to take you on this table. Dinner be damned."

Alessandro's grey eyes darken with lust when I look up at him from under long lashes and flick my tongue across my bottom lip.

What was that I was saying about getting too attached? Ah, fuck it. I want him, and he obviously wants me so why should I fight this attraction anymore. I can have my cake and eat it too. I'll use him as a fuck buddy, as a cuddle buddy, and whatever else, and when it comes time to pull the trigger I'll still be able to do my job. Right?

Yeah, I don't think so either, but a girl can hope.

With my appetite effectively ruined, I stand up from

the table turning towards the hallway. "I'm not hungry... for food," I say over my shoulder after removing my top and throwing it at him.

I didn't think it was possible, but I may have rendered Alessandro speechless. I'm halfway down the hallway to my bedroom when I hear the growl that has my core clenching with anticipation. Then a hard body collides with my back, one strong hand wrapping around my throat and tilting my head back until it's resting against his chest, the other sliding under the waistband of my tiny shorts, seeking out my clit. I've never been gladder that I didn't bother with.

"This what you hungry for, Angel?" he rasps, his breath warm against my ear.

"N-No," I moan when he pinches my clit.

"No? Then, what are you hungry for?"

I swallow hard when he nips and sucks along my jaw. "Your cock."

"What about my cock?"

He wants me to say it out loud. Wants to hear the words from my lips. I was never good at dirty talk. During sexting? Yes. But in person, during the actual act? Not so much. Usually, my mind goes blank, and I have no idea what to say. Not tonight, though. I know what I want, and he can bet his ass that I'm going to tell him exactly what I want... or at least I'll try.

"I-I..."

"You what, Angel?"

I close my eyes, take a deep breath and try again. "I want to taste you."

Alessandro growls, spinning me around to face him. His fingers fist in my long hair, his other hand back around my throat as his lips crash down on mine, demanding the kiss that he wants.

"Then get on your knees and take me out."

His grip on my hair tightens while he forces me down to my knees. With a shaky breath, I undo his belt and pants finding him already hard beneath his boxer-briefs. I pull his underwear down to join his pants in a pool around his ankles.

"Open your mouth, Angel, stick your tongue out."

Alessandro grips the base of his cock and groans, running the head of his cock up and down the length of my tongue. He reaches down and grips my chin with his other hand.

"Wider," he commands.

I relax and open my mouth wider until my jaw begins to ache.

"Good girl," he praises, running both hands through my hair until they're gripping the back of my head and then Alessandro fucks my mouth.

I forgot that he's not just thicker than the average cock, but he's longer too, and I have to relax my throat so that I don't gag as his thrusts become faster. I'm drooling, but that only seems to spur Alessandro on more. He hisses when I hollow out my cheeks and suck hard every time he withdraws. I try not to squirm, but I can't help it. The noises coming from him make my clit throb with anticipation of the hard fucking I know will follow.

"Enough." Alessandro pulls me off his length. Hooking his arms under mine, he hauls me to my feet. His hands are back to gripping the hair at the nape of my neck, and around my throat, as he backs me up until the back of my legs hit the mattress.

Alessandro licks up the side of my face, a growl reverberating through his chest when he nips at my bottom lip. "You're mine, Angel."

My eyes roll back when his mouth finds the secret spot under my ear. My fingers dig into his hips, anchoring me to the here and now. If I let him, Alessandro would consume me; mind, body, and soul.

I need control in my life. Without it, I'm just a trained killer who could go off at any minute. Control is something that I could never give up if I want any semblance of a normal life. But in the bedroom, with Alessandro, I know that I can let go, and he will always be there to catch me. This is one area where I can give up all control to him, and I can be free to just feel.

But what happens when that no longer becomes an option? What happens when there is no more Alessandro? That's not something that I can allow myself to dwell on right now. For now, I can breathe a little easier knowing that Alessandro *is* here, and I'll gladly surrender all my control… to him.

As my back hits the soft sheets of the bed, the only thing on my mind is how unbelievably good his lips feel on my torso as he kisses his way down my middle, dragging my shorts lower with each kiss until he's pulling them free of my legs and tossing them on the floor.

Alessandro stands, kicking out of his own pants and underwear. His fingers gently wrap around my ankle and lift my leg. Lips trailing soft kisses and nips from the inside of my ankle and all the down until he's kneeling in front of me.

"Mine," he growls right before he licks up my slit, sucking my clit between his lips.

My back arches, fingers gripping the sheets at my side.

Alessandro said I was his and that night he claimed me, body and soul, in ways that only existed in my dreams and dark romance novels. He was dangerously close to claiming my heart too, but I refused to acknowledge just *how* close.

That night instead of kicking him out, I fall asleep with my head on his chest and our legs intertwined.

Chapter 11

ALESSANDRO

"**T**ELL ME ABOUT your family."

I had planned on sneaking out in the middle of the night but I must have been more tired than I thought because the next thing I knew I was waking up with Jessika practically wrapped around me like she was afraid I would disappear, and morning light was streaming through the gaps between the curtains in her bedroom.

We've both been awake for a while. I heard the slight change in her breathing several minutes after I woke up. Neither one of us wanted to be the first to move.

"My family?" she asks, her voice still heavy with sleep.

"I want to know more about you, Angel, including where you come from."

She blows out a frustrated breath. I was expecting her to clam up and kick me out with the excuse that this was nothing more than a fuck buddy arrangement. So, I was surprised when she answered.

"The short version? My mother was a drunk until she died when I was five. My father was... barely around, always choosing work and his business dealings over us, and my sister... well, we were close. You could almost say that we were inseparable until her thirteenth birthday."

"What happened on her thirteenth birthday?"

"Our father began training her so that one day she could work in the family business. She became meaner, always pushing me around, yelling at me that I was worthless. I never understood why. Until the day I turned thirteen."

When I look down at her with her head on my chest, hand sprawled over my heart, there's a faraway look in her eyes but then she blinks and it's gone.

"Anyway, after that day our entire lives became one big competition. Who could get the better grades, the hotter boys, who could run faster, jump higher? Who could win our father's affection more? It was exhausting. Then one day I realized that it wasn't the way a family was supposed to be so after I graduated high school I left."

"Thirteen seems a little young for him to already be grooming you to work in the family business."

"There's no such thing to my father. If it were up to him he would've started us sooner, but I guess he made some sort of promise to our mother that he would wait until we were teenagers." She scoffs, moving to sit up and I instantly miss the feel of her soft body against mine. "Thirteen is barely a teenager."

"What is the family business?"

Jessika's entire body stiffens. She swallows hard, avoiding my gaze but she doesn't answer my question. Instead, she reaches for my dress shirt on the floor and slips it on. It's about several sizes too big and on anyone else it would look ridiculous, but she looks fucking edible.

"Coffee?" she asks when she's halfway across the room.

It's glaring obvious there's more to her story but I won't force her to tell me. Not yet.

***
JESSIKA

I wish I can say that I regret giving Alessandro pieces of the puzzle to my past but I don't. That in itself should scare me. This wasn't supposed to go beyond a fun time between the sheets but I found that I want him to know me. I want to share who I am with him. And that's more dangerous to me than getting caught with cold blood on my hands. I can't seem to stop this growing thing between us though and I'm not entirely sure that I want to.

"Come to dinner with me this weekend," Alessandro says as he rounds the corner into the kitchen, wrapping his arms around my middle and pulling me into his chest. His chin resting on the top of my head. "Braxton hosts a family dinner every Sunday night. Come with me this weekend."

"You want me to meet your friends?" I ask against his chest.

"Yes." His hands start roaming my body, over the dip of my lower back and down to squeeze my ass.

"Why?"

Alessandro nips and licks along my neck and I tilt my head to give him better access. His hands massage the cheeks of my ass. If he were to dip under the shorts I'm wearing he would find me already wet for him.

"Just say yes," his breath coasts over my skin and I

shiver in sensation overload with his lips, tongue, teeth, and hands all getting in on the action.

"Yes," I moan. His skilled fingers slipping between my legs and thrusting into my pussy.

Chapter 12

JESSIKA

I'**M NERVOUS AS** fuck as I stand in front of the full-length mirror in my bedroom. I've never met a boyfriend's friends before. *Boyfriend.* Is that what Alessandro and I are now? Boyfriend and girlfriend? Ugh, it sounds so juvenile. After Alessandro cornered me in the kitchen and I agreed to dinner there was no further discussion on why he wanted me to meet his friends so soon when we hadn't even discussed what this thing between us was.

"Mmm, if those jeans were any tighter I'd have to peel you out of them, Angel," Alessandro whispers in my ear from behind me, his hands on my hips pulling me against him so I can feel the outline of his hardening cock against my ass. "Might have to peel you out of them anyway."

I shiver when his fingers brush against the exposed skin between my shirt and the waistband of my jeans. Alessandro smirks at our reflections in the mirror, his hands roaming up my front to cup my breasts under my shirt. I moan, leaning my head back against his chest.

"We'll never make it out of here if you continue doing what you're doing," I breathe.

"And what am I doing, Angel?"

"Making me forget that we have dinner plans with your friends and want to just stay holed up here while we do dirty, dirty things to each other." I wiggle my ass against his growing length and grin when it twitches.

"Christ, that mouth. I can't wait to fuck that pretty mouth when we get home tonight."

My shirt falls back into place against my heated skin when Alessandro removes his hands. I whimper at the sudden loss of heat at my back.

"You could fuck it now," I say, running my tongue along my bottom lip and pulling it between my teeth, my gaze trailing down until they land on the bulge behind his zipper.

"Jessika," Alessandro warns, the dark look he levels at me leaves no room for argument. As much as I want to bait him some more until he unleashes the beast I can see stewing under the surface, I know me meeting Braxton, Klara, and Antonio means more to him than he wants to let on.

"Fine." I stick out my bottom lip in a pout and go about choosing a sweater in case the temperature dips down.

Alessandro ushers me out of my apartment and down the stairs into the guest underground parking stall where his big-ass SUV is parked. Seriously, the thing is like a boat. While he maneuvers us through city traffic I take the time to really admire him. He looks relaxed sitting back in the leather seat, elbow resting on the console between the seat and his right hand draped over the gearshift. His other arm casually draped over the steering wheel. Alessandro is a big guy, but it's his presence that makes him feel larger than life. I can see why Braxton chose him as his Capo. Alessandro demands attention and respect wherever he goes. When you first meet him, he emits this don't *fuck with me* attitude, and anyone would be wise to heed the warning. He keeps his hair trimmed short to his scalp and that only lends to the badass image. That and the leather jacket he's currently wearing.

Twenty minutes later, Alessandro drives up a long, narrow lane lined with trees decorated with small, white flowers. The lane then opens up to reveal a looming mansion with a circular driveway. A mansion is probably describing it mildly. It's a fucking castle. It looks like someone chose a castle in Italy and decided to just pick it up and move it. It puts the three-story house I grew up in to shame. It's gorgeous. And just another reminder that I'm so far beneath these people. I could never measure up to this with my tiny one-bedroom apartment in the city and live off daddy's money. At least for now.

The front door opens just as I'm stepping out of the vehicle and Klara walks out with a huge smile on her face. She doesn't look anything like the girl I got to know in the hospital. The same girl who was held in the room next to mine. She looks healthy… happy. Her ash blonde hair falls in soft waves around her heart-shaped face, her blue eyes glowing with excitement when Alessandro and I make our way over to her and she engulfs me in a bear hug.

"I'm so happy you're here, Jessika," she whispers in my ear before she pulls away then pulls Alessandro into his own hug.

In the car on the way here, he had warned me that Klara was a hugger and that if I wasn't okay with it I should tell her. Honestly, I didn't mind it. I loved it in fact. There were never any signs of affection in my childhood home after my mother died. Frankly, I stopped thinking of it as *home* that day too. It became a building where I ate, rested my head at night and had to put up with my father and sister. Home it was not.

Klara ushers us inside and I have to stop and stare at the entrance way. A marble staircase winds its way up on one side, a chandelier hangs from a high ceiling right above us. Seriously, if that thing falls, there's no hope for either Alessandro or me. I don't care if he is built like the incredible Hulk, we're both going down. Alessandro holds my hand as Klara leads us down open hallway, passed a kitchen that must be every chef's wet dream, and into what I'm assuming is the family room.

There's a man hunched forward on the couch with his elbows resting on his knees as he stares intently at whatever is on the screen. A woman sits next to him, one leg crossed under the other as she smirks at whatever has him riled up. Tattoos decorate her right arm, from her wrists until it disappears beneath the short sleeves of her white t-shirt. A mandala piece peeks out from the hem of her jean shorts too. She's beautiful with her dirty blonde hair thrown up in a haphazard bun atop her head and steel grey-blue eyes outlined in black.

They both notice us standing watching them at the same time, and when the man turns his full attention on me I feel like I've been hit by a mac truck. His stare is so intense I feel like I can't breathe like every inhale and exhale is a challenge. They get to their feet at the same time, like a choreographed routine.

"I'm Sofia, Braxton's cousin." Her painted red lips tip in a smile as she shakes my hand and I instantly know that we'll be good friends. Plus, I want the number of her tattoo artist. The artwork is amazing.

"Jessika," I manage to squeak out in between drooling over the different pieces of art along her arm.

"Don't even think about it," Alessandro growls sensing where my thoughts have gone.

"What?" I ask, batting my lashes up at him.

Alessandro drops my hand, snaking it around my waist and pulling me in closer to his side as he drops his head to whisper in my ear. "The only mark this skin will bear will be my handprint on your ass, Angel." He nips at my earlobe before straightening back up to his full height.

I immediately start cataloging all the places in this mansion where I can drag Alessandro to so that he can carry out his threat. I think I saw an office or a library somewhere along the hallway.

"Have you already forgotten about the little piece on my thigh?" I whisper back and Alessandro growls low so that only I can hear. He's already asked me multiple times what the dagger represents, and each time I've shrugged it off and acted like it was nothing special, just some random design I picked out at the tattoo studio. I hoped he would never pay close attention to the markings though because then I can kiss everything I've worked towards goodbye.

All dirty thoughts of corrupting Alessandro in his best friend's home flee when the mystery man takes my hand in his but instead of shaking it brings my knuckles up to his lips so that he can kiss it.

"Pleasure to meet you." Eyes the bluest I've ever seen stare up at me, I'm momentarily lost in a sea of blue. He only pulls away when I hear a feral growl sounding from my right. Mystery man smirks like he knows exactly what he did to elicit that kind of reaction from Alessandro. "Antonio," he says in a slight Italian accent.

His inky black hair falls over his eyes but he brushes it back, running a hand through the silky strands. He's a couple inches shorter than Alessandro, and definitely built like a brick shithouse, but my man could take him in a fight hands down.

"Antonio," Alessandro growls. "Drop her hand or I'll remove yours."

My eyes round in realization that Antonio had my hand clasped in his the entire time we've been talking… which hasn't been long but from Alessandro reaction you'd think it's been hours.

"I would listen to him, Toni. Alex looks like he's ready for a fight to the death," a voice says from the hall when a man walks toward us, one hand in the pocket of his dress pants, the other wrapped around a glass of amber liquid. I'm assuming this is *the* Braxton De Luca. Don of the Famiglia. I've heard stories about him, and despite my father's intense hatred of the man, I have never seen a picture of him. He's not as tall as Alessandro or Antonio, or as built but with the air of authority swirling around him I guess he doesn't have to be. With one look into his dark eyes and I know exactly why everyone cowers to him.

With one look, it feels like he's seeing straight to the depths of who you are. Like he's seeing all your fears, all your faults, your darkest secrets, and your darkest desires. He sees it all. At least, it feels like he does. It's disarming. I'm not entirely sure why it doesn't surprise me that Braxton De Luca is the only one here in dress pants and dress shirt, but it doesn't. He seems like the type of person who needs to be in control of all things and maybe the suit allows him that.

"Why don't you guys go out back and get the grill

started. The girls can help me with the drinks and sides," Klara says, interrupting the tense stare down between Antonio and Alessandro.

"Grill? Since when do you grill?" Alessandro teases Braxton. All tension is gone.

"Since-fucking-now apparently," he mumbles under his breath, stealing a glance at Klara who just smiles at him innocently.

"Don't burn the meat!" she hollers after their retreating back.

Before I know it, I'm stuck inside with two pairs of curious eyes glued to me like a child's arts and crafts project.

"Drinks? You said there were drinks?" is the first thing out of my mouth before I can stop myself.

Klara and Sofia giggle while each of them loops an arm through one of my own and they lead me into the gorgeous kitchen I caught a glimpse of earlier when Alessandro and I entered the house.

"So… Jessika, tell us about yourself," Sofia says, grabbing a celery stick from a plate of cut vegetables on the island and plopping herself down on a bar height stool.

"Finally decided to use that number, huh?" Klara asks before I can answer Sofia's question.

"Number? What number?" Sofia asks, looking between Klara and me.

"I gave her Alessandro's number two years ago. Guess she never used it until now," Klara shrugs, going about gathering bottles of wine and bourbon then setting the bottles on the counter in front of Sofia.

"Oh, shit," Sofia's grey-blue widen in alarm. "Does Alex know that?"

Klara shrugs again as she lines up three wine glasses

and three glass tumblers. She stares at the tumblers, biting her lip as she thinks and then takes one away before filling the remaining ones. "Braxton already has a drink out there," she says by way of explanation.

When she's done pouring everyone's drinks, and placing the wine bottle back on the counter and locks eyes with me. It's then I realize that their back and forth volleying of questions has stopped and they're both looking at me expectantly.

Oh crap, I knew this was bound to happen but I hadn't actually thought about what I was going to say when asked about myself. I can't exactly blurt out that I was born into the Bratva, and not just born into but that my father was the head honcho. That I had the furthest thing from a normal childhood, and oh yeah, I was trained to become an assassin starting at the age of thirteen. Yeah... *that* wouldn't go over very well, especially considering who's house we're standing in.

So I shrug and give the usual answer I always give. "There's not much to tell. I had an okay childhood. My dad was never around, even before my mom died, so I pretty much raised myself." Then because I can pretty much guarantee what questions came next – do you have any siblings? Or I'm so sorry. How'd she die? - I turn my attention to Klara. "You're looking good, Klara. Happy." I note with a warm smile.

She turns a shade of red only rivaled by Sofia's lip color, her pale eyes searching for something over the back of Sofia's head and out the huge window overlooking the backyard. A soft smile lifts the corners of her lips when she finds what... or who she's looking for. "I am," she says almost dreamily. "Braxton is..." - she pauses- "he can be a hard man sometimes but I wouldn't change who he is. He came into my life at a time I needed him the most and I think the same is true for him."

A silent moment passes while we allow her to stare at her man and get lost in whatever memories have her eyes glazing over.

"Ugh, enough with the fairytale, heart-eyes stuff," Sofia whines, popping a cherry tomato in her mouth. "I want to know the dirty. Is it true about the size of a man's hands?" She waggles her eyebrows at me and I can't fight the belly laugh that rumbles through me.

"No comment," I wheeze, trying to catch my breath.

"Awh, C'mon! Spill the dirt, Jess. I'm single, I need to live vicariously through you cause there's no way in hell I'm living vicariously through her," she tips her head indicating Klara. "That's just… ew," she shivers. "I can't even go there. That's a whole lot of nope," she says popping the p.

"Sorry, Sofia. I never kiss and tell," I say with a wink and that earns me a pout from Braxton's cousin.

I chance a glance over Sofia's head while the two of them go about discussing other things and catch Alessandro's eyes staring back at me through the pane of glass. A smirk pulls at his lips, his eyes blazing with heat and promise of what's to come once we get back to his place. A shiver runs through me and I cannot wait.

Alessandro ends the connection all too soon but by the sudden snarl of his lips I'm guessing the conversation he's having with Braxton and Antonio isn't a good one.

I tune back into my conversation with Sofia and Klara just in time to hear Klara say, "…anniversary of his brother's death."

"Whose brother?" I ask.

"Alessandro," Sofia answers automatically and then slaps a hand over her mouth. I'm assuming because she wasn't supposed to tell me that tidbit of information, which is confirmed by the look of horror on Klara's face.

"Alessandro has a brother?"

"Um…" Sofia hums, looking everywhere but at me.

"He did," Klara says hesitantly, gauging my reaction.

"Oh," I shrug, breaking off a piece of celery stick.

"You're not going to ask what happened?" Sofia asks with a lifted brow.

"Nope. Not really my place to ask. If Alessandro wanted me to know he'll tell me."

The two women eye me wearily but must sense that I'm saying is the truth because they go back to talking and preparing sides. Well, Klara goes back to preparing sides while Sofia and I watch. We did ask her if she wanted help but she shooed us and said she had it all handled. I wasn't complaining. Me and kitchens don't have a good relationship. I'll burn water for crying out loud.

We each grab a side dish and carry it out to a big cast iron table with glass top in the backyard. Alessandro draws me into his side when I try and pass him to go help Sofia and Klara bring the drinks out.

"Having fun, Angel?"

I wrap my arms around his middle and smile up at him. "I am." And it's the truth. I haven't felt this accepted anywhere in a very long time.

"Good," he says kissing my forehead. I think this is the first time anyone has ever done that and I sort of like it. Okay, I love it.

"I know something we could do that would make it even more fun though," I say, waggling my eyebrows playfully.

Alessandro immediately grabs my hand, placing his open beer on the closest table and pulls me alongside him back into the house. I giggle when he pushes open what looks like an office door and pulls me inside. Slamming my back up against the door as soon as it's closed.

"These jeans look like they're too hot for this weather, Angel, I may have to strip you of them to cool you down," he rasps between kisses along my neck. My jeans already undone before the words have fully left his mouth.

Alessandro kisses along the tops of my breasts, hooking his fingers in the waistband of my pants and pushing my jeans and underwear down in one. He kneels in front of me, yanking the pants and underwear off one leg and then hitching that same leg over his shoulder.

"Can you be quiet, Angel?" he asks in between licks up my slit, his tongue teasing my wet entrance before each lick.

"I-I can try," I pant, fingers curling over his head.

"Good, because if Braxton finds us in his office I'll never hear the end of it. Now, give me this pussy."

Alessandro swirls his tongue around my clit and then sucks it in his mouth as his hitches my leg higher up his shoulder. His teeth graze the sensitive bud and I buck my hips, arching my back off the door. My grip on his head tightens and I hold him to my sex when his thrusts one finger inside me and then another and another until his filling me.

"Alessandro," I moan, my hips bucking faster against his face.

His fingers curl, finding the spot that drives me wild

while he eats me like I'm his last fucking meal. My body pulls tight and then the sweetest of highs takes over as I come crashing down. My entire body shuddering with the effects of the orgasm Alessandro gave me.

He helps me back into my jeans, slapping my ass before pulling me into a kiss. I wish, not for the first time, that were back at his place because then I could jump him right now and ride him like a slut on a bucking bull at a country bar.

***

ALESSANDRO

After making sure our clothes are back in place and nothing out of order, a red file folder with a yellow sticky note on Braxton's desk catches my eye, but what has my feet moving toward it is the name in black ink handwritten across the note. Vincent Ferrara. My father. Why would Braxton have a file on my father?

"You okay?" Jessika asks, her hands sprawled across my back.

I snatch up the file before she can get a good look at it and fold it in half. Slipping it in the waistband behind my back when I turn back around to face her.

"I'm good, Angel," I reply, kissing her forehead. "Let's go get some food."

***

JESSIKA

When Braxton has declared that the meat is done, we all gather around the table. Our plates filled high with all sorts of grilled meats from chicken, ribs, steak, and even burgers - which I was told was by Sofia's request-

and various sides like macaroni salad, potato salad, even garlic bread, and of course the plate of cut-up vegetables.

Conversation flows easily while we all dig into the food. Everyone seems surprised that Braxton hasn't managed to burn the food but instead the meat is perfectly cooked. I take that to mean he's not so great in a kitchen either or he just never bothers to cook.

As the food gets eaten and the drinks flow, I feel myself relaxing more and more and lowering my guard a little. It feels so good to laugh, and not just any laugh but full belly laughs. I don't think I've ever laughed this much or had this much fun.

Something still nags at the back of my mind though. I can't help but wonder why Alessandro never mentioned that he had a brother. I mean, I know it's kind of hypocritical of me because I've never told him about my sister either but for some reason, it hurts more than it should knowing that he's keeping parts of himself from me.

That's like the pot calling the kettle black, isn't it?

I shake off the thought and decide to leave it alone. Alessandro will tell me when he's good and ready to tell me. Right? Right.

***

Wrong.

It's been a week since we had dinner at Braxton and Klara's house, and Alessandro still hasn't told me about his brother.

Get a grip, Jessika. You already knew about his brother so what difference does it make?

The difference is that I keep wishing Alessandro will

tell me himself. I remind myself that a week isn't long at all and maybe Alessandro is just waiting until we know each other a little better first before he tells me. That's what goes through my head, but what comes out my mouth one evening while we're sitting on his sofa watching TV is the polar opposite.

"Why didn't you tell me you had a brother?"

If I didn't think the topic was off limits before, I do now. Alessandro's body closes up like Fort Knox. His posture turns rigid, jaw ticking, and I swear the vein popping on his forehead may actually burst.

"Never mind," I try to backtrack, "I shouldn't have brought it up. I'm sorry." I try to settle back against his chest but he's so stiff that I end up moving to the other side of the sofa and curling my legs up under me.

"It's not a pretty story, Jess," he says, blowing out a breath and I can tell it's taking everything in him to release the tension that has him coiled so tight.

"Alex, you don't have to…"

"He died when we were boys," he interrupts me, turning those grey eyes on me. "You sure you want to hear this?"

"Only if you want me to," I reply honestly.

Alessandro shakes his head, "you'll never look at me the same way again, Angel."

"You can't possibly know that."

"Si," he says, "I do because my parents never looked at me the same way again after it happened."

I sit up straighter, uncurling my legs and dropping my feet to the floor. I'm sensing that whatever it is he's about to tell me could very well impact the way I view him and our relationship, but I already decided a while ago that I wasn't giving him up. To hell with my father and everyone else.

I move closer to him, placing a hand on one his that are balled into fists on his bouncing leg.

"I killed my brother with a tree branch," he grits out.

Everything inside me stills, but I don't remove my hand from where it's covering his. That was not what I was expecting when he said he killed his brother. *With a tree branch?* What the fuck?

"I don't know exactly what happened. All I remember is waiting for Johnny to come play with me in the treehouse our father had just built for us, but he was younger and the ladder was still hard for him to climb so he always refused to play with me."

Alessandro's jaw clenches again, any harder and I'm afraid he won't have any teeth left back there.

"The next thing I know our mother is kneeling in front of me, yelling for my dad and asking me what I did. I couldn't remember a damn thing, Jess. Even to this day, I can't remember anything that happened in between those two events, except thinking that he didn't want to play with me."

I'm almost afraid to ask but I want to know. "How did... what did..." I swallow and try again. "What did your parents do after they found him?"

"That's the fucked-up part. That was the day I learned how to get rid of a body. I may have accidentally found the path, but my father lit the way to me becoming what I am now." His lips lift in a snarl like those very words leave a bitter taste in his mouth. "This is what you get with me, Jessika," he says turning to face me. "I do the Famiglia's dirty work. Anything they ask of me, I do it. Nothing is off limits. And I killed my own brother."

He's trying to scare me away before we even have a chance, but it won't work because while yes, that is fucked up and I briefly think back to try and recognize any sociopathic tendencies I may have overlooked, I have also seen and done my fair share of fucked up things.

I know enough about this man to know that if he could he would go back and change what he did, but ultimately that path led him to Braxton which led him to me.

"You can't scare me, Alex," I tell him, snuggling back into his side and inhaling the comforting scent of pure man. I suspect that there's more he's not telling me but if I push him Alessandro will close up even more.

After his confession, Alessandro takes me to bed and proves how much I was right. He's no less a monster than I am. Sex with Alessandro has always been rough and fast... marking. But tonight, tonight it's all slow, sensual touches, soft kisses, licks and little nips. Alessandro spends hours bringing me to the brink only to back off until my threatening orgasm subsides only to build me back up again. And finally, when early morning light begins shining through the curtains of his room, does he allow the waves to crash over me.

"What's your number one fantasy?" I ask him, my head on his chest, our legs entangled and both of us fighting the post-orgasmic slumber.

"You really want to know?" Alessandro counters, drawing little circles on my exposed shoulder.

"I do," I say, resting my chin on his chest and peering up at him.

"I want to watch as another guy fucks you then I want both of us to double penetrate you. Me in your tight, wet pussy while he continues to fuck your ass and after you cum so hard you think you're going to die, I'm going to fuck his ass until I cum and he'll spill his load in your gorgeous ass. And you'll take it all because I tell you to."

I shiver, my thighs clenching. I'm already wet again from that little visual. "Okay," I say, breathlessly.

"Okay?" Alessandro asks, an eyebrow raised.

"I-I want that too."

"Turn over and go to sleep, Jessika," Alessandro grunts, stopping my hand from its descent under the covers and towards its target that's currently pitching a tent under the duvet. Once I'm on my side, Alessandro spoons up against my back, a hand coasting down my belly to cup my sex.

"This pussy is mine and mine alone. I'm the only one who gets to fuck it," he growls, nipping at my ear. "Now be a good girl and go to sleep."

Chapter 13

"**I CAN'T DO** it anymore, Mel," I say into the phone the minute I hear the call connect.

"Can't do it anymore? Can't do what anymore?" She asks, sleep clouding her voice and making me momentarily feel bad for calling her at – I check my watch – seven in the morning. Oy, I'm a bad friend. Mel never wakes up before nine.

"My mission... my mark."

Mel snorts sounding more awake. "Honey, I think it's too late for that. You're already doing your mark."

"Ugh," I groan. "That's not what I meant and you know it."

She giggles, "I know. I'm just teasing you," she says before the line goes quiet and everything turns serious. "Then don't do it, Jess. You're not his puppet. Stand up for what you want once in your life and tell your father to go to hell."

This is why I called my best friend. She doesn't like my father, never has even though they've only met once. She's got my back... always. I knew before I called her that I was most likely going to tell my dad to shove his revolver up his ass, but I needed that extra push, that extra sign letting me know I was doing the right thing. The self-martyr thing most likely but the right thing nonetheless.

"I think I'm going to do it, Mel, I'm going to sever all ties with the Bratva."

"Good," she yawns. "It's about bloody time too."

Did I mention how much I love my best friend? Well, I do.

"Oh, and Jess," she says right before I hang up. "Try not to get killed."

"Love you too, Melanie."

"Love you, boo," she yawns into the phone again before hanging up.

No sooner have I hit the little red button on my screen ending the call, does it ring again with a private number. A ball of lead hits heavy in my belly because only one person ever calls me from a private number. Each time Amanda has called it's been an unknown number, but every time *he's* called it's from a private number. And every single time it's been because he has added another mark to my list.

"You said one more," I answer the call. My grip tightens around the phone until my knuckles turn white.

"Consider this a guarantee," my father's deep voice comes through loud and clear.

"A guarantee?"

"Do this one extra and your retirement from the Bratva will be a guarantee. That is still what you want, isn't it? A clean start away from the Romanov name?"

"Yes." I could legally change my name. I could move to the other side of the world but unless my father made it clear that I was out and untouchable I would always be looking over my shoulder wondering if that'll be the day the sins of my past catch up to me.

"Then do it, Jessika. You'll find all the information in the folder and I expect an update by morning." With that, my father hangs. No goodbye as per usual.

With a resounding sigh, I lean back against the leather back of the desk chair, eyeing the folder that was just delivered that morning with weary contempt. If I do this... if I do this one extra job for the Bratva what would stop them from adding one more after this one is done, and one more after that. There could always be just one more hit. But if I don't do it and my father wasn't lying about it being the last... well, I'm fucked either way. Plus, I could use a stress reliever that didn't involve a few rounds of dirty sex with Alessandro. My body was sore and tired and well used after last night.

A smile tugs at the corner of my mouth at the memory of Alessandro's hands, lips, and tongue on my body. The way his dirty words had a direct link to my core. My thighs clench at the memory and in anticipation of more to come later on. But first, I needed to take care of this extra job.

Reaching for the folder, I flip it open and begin studying everything there is to know about my mark. Father always was very accurate in the information he gathered about anyone. Everything was laid out in a neat little bow for me, from where they worked and lived to what time they got up in the morning, what they had to eat that day and even who they fucked. This one was no different, and it looked like he was closer than I anticipated.

I read over all the information a third and fourth time, and when I'm confident that I know everything there is to know about Daniel Price, I shut the folder and feed it through the paper shredder in the far corner of my office slash guest room slash library.

***

Daniel Price looks like sex on a stick in his dark designer suit as he enters the bar. An arrogant smirk on his gorgeous mouth as he slaps hands with a couple men at a high-top table before joining them. Before that first morning I woke up next to Alessandro, I would've been all over Mr. Price. Used my body to seduce him like every arrogant prick before him but with him, I would've gone all the way and when his defenses were down when he was coming inside me, that's when I would've dragged my blade across his throat.

The smell of sex and death permeating the air as I gathered up my clothes, careful not to leave anything else behind… well, anything more than the biological evidence on the sheets, and then left the classy hotel room which he would've paid for. Oh, I wouldn't be worried about any DNA evidence, that was one thing when being the princess of the Bratva came in handy. One phone call and it would look like the room had never been used.

That would've been before Alessandro wormed his way into my heart and decided to put up shop. Even though we hadn't put a label on whatever this is, and even though shit was complicated with my job, I can't bring myself to betray him any further by sleeping with another man. That's when I decide to enact plan b.

I remove the hair tie holding my hair back and shake it out, long, thick, waves cascading down my back. Grabbing the apron I saw their waitress throw over the bar before she went on her break. I swipe the tray with his drink from the bar top but not before adding an extra little something and saunter over to his table.

"Whiskey on the rocks," I lower my voice to a raspy timber and keep my gaze down, hiding my features behind a curtain of dark hair, while I set the glass down on the table in front of him. I walk away before he has a chance to strike up a conversation, tossing the try and apron on the far corner of the bar and retaking my seat in the darkened corner, away from prying eyes and where I have a perfect view of the table.

The powder won't take effect immediately, he'll be two or three drinks deep before he'll notice that something isn't right. His chest will start to feel like there's a heavy weight on top of it, each breath will become harder and harder until he's choking on it. And then his body will just... give up.

It's the first and only time I've had to resort to a less... hands-on approach to taking out a mark and I have to admit it's not as satisfying as dragging my blade across their skin or seeing my bullet between their eyes, though it is still captivating to watch.

I make my exit while everyone in the busy bar rushes over to Price and someone yells to call nine-one-one. There's really no point though, by the time the ambulance arrives Daniel Price will be long gone.

It's done

I toss the phone in a nearby planter box as I step outside and onto the sidewalk to hail a cab.

Chapter 14

ALESSANDRO

LAST NIGHT'S CONVERSATION with Jessika had me remembering the folder I took from Braxton's home office Sunday night. I close the door to my office and pour myself a stiff drink of bourbon from the decanter behind my desk. I reach into the usually locked top drawer of my desk and pull out the offending folder, slapping it down in front of me.

I finish my first drink and pour another. Unsure of whether or not I want to know what's in the folder. The writing looks like it could belong to Lukas, Braxton's father, but I'll never know until I open it. What could the De Luca's possible have on my father or my family for that matter? My head is pounding from the amount of pressure on my jaw from the number of times I've clenched and unclenched my jaw debating with myself if I should open it or slip it back it back into Braxton's office without him knowing.

"Fuck it."

I slam back the rest of my drink, flipping open the folder. But I was not prepared for what greeted me. There are sheets and sheets of printed paper, a tape recording, banking information, safety deposit box information, and keys. Years and Years of information on my father stare up at me in printed black ink. The type of information he probably didn't want to be exposed, the type of information worthy of blackmail. Apparently, my meeting Braxton back in high school was no coincidence, and according to one of the sheets of paper, my father had been working for the Mafia since Braxton's father took over as Don from his father.

Dad was their hired hitman, except it looks like he had an anger problem that they couldn't control especially when his drinking began getting out of control. A brief vision of him walking out the back door with a bottle of jack hits me but I shake it off. His alcohol abuse hit an all-time low in 1987 when Lukas tried to replace his position within the Famiglia because he could no longer trust my father.

1987 was the year I killed my brother, my vision starts to blur but I don't know if it's from the drinks I've had, the new information about my father, or the memories trying to creep back up. I shut my eyes and breathe through my nose. Something nags me in the back of my mind, like a memory I've been successful in forgetting.

When I turn the page, there's no more ignoring why that date and that vision of my father with a bottle of alcohol are trying to make their way to the forefront of my mind and there's no more forgetting.

"Johnny!" I yell, scanning the backyard for my three-year-old brother, but he's not answering.

I told him to wait for me, that I just needed to go pee and then I would be back and would help him into the treehouse this time. I knew he was still afraid of climbing the ladder because he was still so small, but that's why he had me. I was his big, older brother. I would protect him.

My father stumbles down from the ladder of the treehouse, his foot catching in one of the bottom steps and he barely catches himself before he falls.

"Dad!" I call him. "Have you seen Johnny? We were supposed to play in the treehouse today."

My dad ignores me, stumbling passed. He almost falls over pulling open the screen door to the house but he manages and then it slams shut behind him, leaving a stench of stale alcohol in his wake. I may only be six-years-old but I know that smell is only noticeable when dad's been drinking. He seems to be doing a lot of drinking lately. Ma said it was just his way of relaxing after a long day at work and that we should leave him and alone and let him be. But dad hasn't been to work this week. He's just been sitting in his chair watching the wrestling again.

I want to be a wrestler when I grow up. They're tough and scary, just like my dad. My red toy car catches my eye and I bend to pick it up, checking it over while making my way to the bottom of the treehouse. I pocket it in my shorts and begin the short climb. I don't know why Johnny thinks it's hard. It's not hard, he's just small. When I pull myself up through the door, I see Johnny lying in the middle.

"Johnny, you were supposed to wait for me," I say but he doesn't move. "Johnny?" I ask moving towards him, sitting on my knees so that I can get closer and shove at his chest, trying to get him to move but he still doesn't, and when I pull my hands back they're sticky and red. I look back at my little brother in shock and that's when I see why he won't move. There's a tree branch sticking out of his little body.

"Johnny!" I yell, pushing him again. "Ma! Ma!" I scream, hoping she'll hear me. Sometimes our ma has hearing like an eagle and other times not so much. I hope today is one of those days where she's an eagle…

I slap the folder closed and push away from the desk like it's on fire. There's no fucking way. No fucking way is my father responsible for my brother's death. It was me. I did it. Didn't I? My father looked and acted sober when my Ma called for him and he picked up my brother's little body. Then I remember his eyes when he began reaching for me. At first, I didn't know what it was that I saw in his eyes that day, I was a child who was still learning about the world around him, but now as a man looking back on it, I recognize that it wasn't regret for what he had done but fear that I would rat about seeing him stumbling from the treehouse minutes before I discovered my brother's dead body.

"Fuck!" I roar, swiping everything off my next in one shove, and racking a hand over my head. My father killed my fucking brother and made it look like I had done it. I needed answers and not from a goddamn computer printout, but Lukas De Luca was no longer alive and if I ever saw my father again I was going to kill him for making me go through life believing I was a brother killer. The only other person that left was Braxton, and I would bet my left nut that he knew exactly what had gone down that day thirty-one years ago because I can guarantee that Lukas never kept his son in the dark about any of the business.

I find Braxton running on the treadmill in his basement gym. I get on the one next to his without a word and match his stride. We run side by side for forty more minutes without saying a word to each other. I needed to burn off the extra adrenaline running through me when I first got here because if I hadn't, I would've had him up against the wall with my hands bunched in the front of his shirt.

"Spit it out, Alessandro," he finally says, grabbing a

sweat towel and moving over to the weight bench. "I know you found the folder."

"How long have you known?" I ask taking a stance at the head of the bench so that I can spot him.

"How long have I known that you took the folder? Or how long have I known about your father?"

"My father," I grunt, folding my arms across my chest but staying loose enough so that if he starts struggling with the weight I can jump in and help him.

"I just found out. That's why the folder was on my desk. I hadn't had a chance to go through everything that was in my father's possession until recently. That folder was among his personal things."

"Tell me what happened."

"Haven't you read the contents? It's all there."

"I wanted to hear it from you," I say, switching spots with him and taking a seat on the bench.

"Your father came to my dad with the story that you had accidentally stabbed Johnny with a tree branch. My father didn't believe him. Vincent had a reputation for skirting the truth. My father told him he either came clean or the Famiglia wouldn't help him. He confessed to following Johnny up the treehouse in a drunken stupor. According to him, that's when he blacked out and when he came to his hand was wrapped around the branch that was in Johnny's chest."

"Jesus Christ." The bar clanks against the stand and I push myself into a sitting position, elbows resting on my knees.

"My father agreed to help him on one condition. That he move your family to Canada where the Famiglia could keep an eye on him, and that you attend my school. My father wasn't taking any chances with your safety, Alessandro. That was the only way he could ensure that you didn't meet the same feat as your brother."

"So, I didn't kill my brother?"

"You think my father would've taken you in if you did, Alessandro? You think I would've accepted you if you had?" Braxton shakes his, hands on his hips as he breathes hard after his last set. "You didn't kill Johnny, Alessandro," he says in confirmation.

"You said you didn't know until recently."

"I didn't," Braxton says, picking up a dumbbell. "But I heard the rumors circling around the soldiers about you and your family and why your father decided to join us in Canada. I also knew that if any of it was true, my father never would've accepted you as his own," he grunts, finishing his set and placing the weights back on the rack. "And make no mistake, Alessandro, you were like a son to my father. It's why he also left you some of his fortune."

"I never wanted any of his money," I say, grabbing my own sweat towel and wiping my face.

"I know," Braxton answers, patting me on the back as he walks past. "Let's head up to the office. I have something else I need to discuss with you."

***

"How well do you know Jessika?" Braxton asks once we're back in his home office.

"Not very well," I say, making myself a drink at the bar before taking a seat across from his desk. "We fuck that's it." That's a lie. I'm falling for her and that scares the ever-living shit out of me. I don't do love. The last person I loved, I killed.

Braxton relaxes back in his leather chair and crosses

an ankle over his knee. Anybody outside of the Famiglia might look at him and see a picture of cool, calm, and collected. But I've known this man for twenty years and I can practically see the storm clouds brewing.

He reaches over and pushes a file that was sitting on his desk closer to me to pick up. The name Romanov sprawled across the top in black ink.

"What does Jessika have to do with the Bratva?"

"Open it," he says, and I do. Then my world comes to a screeching halt.

Played.

I've been played like a fucking puppet with Jessika pulling the strings. I invited her into my house, introduced her to the people I hold most dear in this life and it was all just some illusion. None of it was real.

"I'll take care of it," I growl, throwing the file back on his next and far enough away from me like that would somehow make the information in the file any less of the truth.

"Don't fuck this up, Alessandro. I'm counting on you to fix this."

"Consider it done." I slam back the rest of my drink and exit Braxton's office.

I spend the next two hours in the gym in the basement of my new house until my muscles are screaming in protest and I'm drenched in sweat. The bitch thought she could get the drop on me. Take me by surprise. That we wouldn't figure out what she was up to until the last minute... *my* last minute.

For fuck's sake, Alessandro, she's just another pussy. You can go out tonight and find another one. She's nothing special. Do what you've become so good at doing. Do what the mafia pays you to do. Bury the bitch.

With a renewed determined, I shower and dress

grabbing my wallet and car keys on the way out. She has no fucking idea what she just unleashed.

Jessika Tomlinson aka Jessika Romanov is as good as dead.

"Jessika!" I pound a fist on her apartment door not giving a fuck if the neighbors hear or complain. I don't stop pounding until the door swings open. Jessika stands on the other side, hair wet like she just got out of a shower. She looks fucking adorable and if I wasn't so fucking mad I'd fuck her up against the wall. Hell, maybe I still will for old times' sake.

When those emerald eyes lock with mine, my heart screams *mine*, but I immediately shake it off and stalk towards her until her back is pressed up against a wall in the living room.

***

JESSIKA

When I opened the door, it didn't take me long to realize that Alessandro knew. He knew everything. The anger and betrayal are rolling off him in waves but it was his eyes that truly gutted me and the already half-smoked cigarette dangling from between the fingers of the hand not raised to bang on my door. He said he had stopped the habit years ago. Was that a lie or was I the one who drove him to take up the habit again?

His chest heaves with every heavy breath, fists clenching and unclenching at his sides. I knew this was coming. Have been anticipating the day when it would happen, but never would I expect the tears threatening to spill from my eyes, or the way my heart just seized in my chest. As fucked up as my life has been, I've never regretted a damn thing. Until now.

"Is it true?"

I don't trust my voice to not break so I simply nod, then flinch when his fist hits the wall beside the door.

Alessandro walks me back until I'm pressed up against another wall. A hand coming up to rest beside my head on the painted surface.

"Today the day you going to kill me, Jess?" The other hand, still holding his burning cigarette, trails down the exposed skin between my breasts.

I don't answer him. I don't know how he found out or who told him. I had tried putting it off as long as I could, but soon my sister will be here to finish the job if I couldn't.

One more job.

One more job and then *he* promised me I would be free of the family. I refused to be a pawn in my father's game anymore. That didn't go over to well with my father. Once he has his eyes set on something, he'll do anything to get it. Including threatening his own daughter with her life. See, daddy dearest is the head of the Bratva. We were another one of the biggest crime families in Canada… the other being De Luca and the Italian Mafia. But dad didn't just want to be *one* of the best, he wanted to be *the* best. And the only way he could see to do that was to take out Braxton by destroying everything he held dear and everyone close to him. Including Klara and Alessandro.

Dante and Giovanni were supposed to play a big role in that by kidnapping Klara, and they did by convincing Braxton that Dante wanted to run the Famiglia. But they failed when they got themselves killed at the hands of Braxton himself. I was one of the girls Braxton and his men found in the shitty run-down building.

This is where my story gets all kinds of fucked. Up until then, I had been an innocent, naïve nineteen-year-old who thought the world was her oyster. I was going to leave the Bratva behind and go off to college on the other side of the world where I never had to look back. If I ever thought my family would allow that, I was sorely mistaken. It was made pretty clear to me that I was expected to do the family's dirty work. Just like my sister, Amanda. It wasn't until I refused that I saw who my father really was. He handed me over to Dante and his men like I meant nothing to him and told them to do with me what they wanted. And they did. Repeatedly.

One year. Three-hundred-sixty-five days.

I lost my innocence that year. I lost any hope of a future outside of the family. I lost my will to live. Then Alessandro saved me along with the other girls. It was a cruel joke that I was now tasked with killing the man who saved my life, the man I wasn't falling in love with because I had already fallen. The man who knew I had betrayed him.

I hiss as the burning ash at the end of his cigarette touches my skin. Alessandro smirks, taking a drag of the cigarette and exhaling the smoke in my face. His hand coming down to rest on the other side of my head, successfully caging me in.

His nose runs up the curve of my neck, his lips brushing against my ear with his next words. "When it's time for you to do it, drive the knife through my heart. That way I can look into your eyes when you realize that you just killed your only hope at redemption."

I can't hold in the sob threatening its way up my throat any longer. I duck under his arm and do the one thing I've become so good at.

I run.

I'd be back. I'd have to. It was my apartment. But for now, I jump into the driver's side of my jeep and I gun it. Not caring where I'm going just feeling the need to drive as far and as fast as the vehicle will allow. Today was another failed attempt to do what I needed to do.

I pull up to a red light, the decision to go right or left staring me in the face. Sometimes it amazed me that life could find little ways of making you re-think everything in your life. Like right now for instance. If I go left it'll eventually lead to the border. I could be free from my father's hold for a little while until he realizes where I've gone and catches up with me. He's a mob boss… it's inevitable. Going left also takes me away from Alessandro. If I choose right, that takes me in the opposite direction. Eventually, it'll lead to the trans-Canada highway and closer to my father. Either way, I end up losing the man I've fallen in love with.

Then there's a third option. Could I do it? Could I kill the love of my life in order to free myself?

With a decision made I turn right, ignoring the honks from the vehicle I just cut off.

***

With my head held high and a renewed determination, I walk through the front door of my childhood home and straight towards the back of the grand house where my father's office is located. I don't bother knocking. I won't give him the satisfaction of being able to turn me way or making me wait until my resolve to do this today fades. I push open the heavy door and come face to face with my father and uncle.

"Jessika." My father's voice booms across the room and I have to fight against the shudder that threatens to race up my body. It's not the good kind of shudder either... the one that Alessandro always manages to elicit from me.

"Father." I tip my chin in acknowledgment. "Uncle."

My uncle stands, his six-two frame somehow more commanding in this room than that of my father sitting behind his ornate desk.

"Nikolay." he stands from his seat, doing the buttons on his suit jacket before shaking hands with my father then turning to me. "Jessika, you get more and more stunning every time I see you," he says, placing his hands on my shoulders and then bringing me in for a hug.

There were times my uncle was more a father to me than my own. He wasn't cold and closed off when he came to visit. He showered us with hugs, brought us gifts, but most importantly he made us laugh. That never changed when I started my training if anything his visits became more frequent. They were the only things that got me through the worst of it. Knowing that my uncle Vik was coming to visit was all the motivation I needed to get me through a week of hell in this house.

"Thank you, Uncle."

"Don't be a stranger, Jessika," he admonishes placing a kiss on the top of my head and then turning to leave. I feel guilty for not going to see him after I was discharged from the hospital two years ago, but after what my father demanded of me and the reality of what my life had become I just couldn't bring myself to. I wanted to believe that Vik had nothing to do with the family business but I knew that he did. He was the only one my father trusted.

'Is it done?" my father asks as soon as the door closes shut behind my uncle.

"Hello to you too, father." I walk towards his desk and stop in front of it refusing to take a seat in one of the chairs. I need every advantage I can get, and it may seem stupid but having to look down on him as he sat behind his desk gives me the illusion of that advantage. "But to answer your question, no, it is not done."

Anger flashes behind my father's dark eyes, a vein popping on his forehead as he tries to reign himself in. For a brief moment, I wonder how the hell I could possibly be related to this monster. The only thing that comforts me is the thought that maybe I took after my mother. I have her looks, maybe I have her strong will as well. Amanda sure as hell doesn't take after our mother. She's our father's identical in every way.

Fuck, here goes nothing. I take a deep breath, round my shoulders and do something that could cost both Alessandro and I our lives.

"I refuse to do it. I *won't* kill him."

My father pushes to his feet, his palms planted firmly on the polished surface of the desk. "You *will* do it," he seethes. "And you will do it tonight!"

"No," my voice is firm when I stare my father down.

"You dare defy me!"

I flinch when his fists hit the desk with a resounding thud, but I refuse to back down.

"I owe you nothing, father. I never wanted to be part of this. Alessandro is no threat to you. Let him live."

Dark eyes narrow like they're trying to see through

me and part of me always thought that they could.

"Ебать! *Fuck!*" my father swears under his breath. "You love him." It wasn't a question but I find myself answering him anyway.

"I do not love him."

My father rounds the desk and walks towards me until there's nothing separating us. He grips my chin hard, tipping it up until I'm looking straight into eyes as black as his soul. "Do not lie to me. You love the Italian."

I don't answer him this time but whatever he sees in my eyes must be answer enough because he takes a step back right before his palm connects with the side of my face leaving white-hot heat in its place. My father grabs me by my throat and squeezes. My hand's paw at his wrists, nails scratching against his skin.

"You owe your life to this family. You will do as I say or you will die alongside those Italian scum." He releases his grip and I fall to my knees, panting, trying to suck in as much needed air as I can.

"Love is for the weak, Jessika. I'll make it easy for you though, daughter. Either kill the Capo or I'll kill you. Now, get out of my face and go do your job."

I scramble to my feet, tears blurring my vision as I race out of his office and out the front door of the house, not stopping until I'm in my car with all the doors locked. I'm such an idiot. What did I expect? That I could go there, stare my father down and he would just accept my demands?

You owe your life to this family.

I was stupid to think that I could ever earn my freedom from this family. My father had no intentions of letting me walk away, regardless of if I killed Alessandro or not. He would just find another reason why he needed me. One more job. One more hit.

Love is for the weak, Jessika.

Maybe he had a point though. Ever since I gave in to my body's demand for Alessandro I've gotten soft. Before meeting him I would've had no problems with killing someone after fucking them. It was just the way the game worked. But now... now the game has changed.

I'm taking my life back, starting with Alessandro.

***
ALESSANDRO

The fucking Bratva. She was the daughter of the Russian boss.

Betrayed.

Humiliated.

The fucking tattoo on her thigh should've given her away but every time I got close to it, she was naked and I had a different mission in mind. But the tattoo... it was a Bratva tattoo, one that meant the bearer has killed before.

I drop down on the leather sofa of my new living room, the ice clinking in the glass as it dangles from my hand. I was in love with a fucking Romanov. The vilest crime family. They make the De Luca's look like angels.

Angel.

"Fuck!" I roar, my glass flying across the room. I didn't bother getting up to clean it. The glass tumbler was slowing me down anyway. I pick up the bottle and take a healthy swig and then another until there's nothing left. All while ignoring the ping of various text messages coming from my phone.

The alcohol was effective in luring me into a deep

sleep, but I still dreamt of Jessika. The way her body felt against mine, the way her emerald eyes lightened to an impossible shade of green when she laughed. And I knew that despite her wanting to kill me, her love for me was real and I would love her until my last breath until she pulled that trigger.

Chapter 15

I COULDN'T TAKE it anymore. The pressure. The guilt. The gaping hole in my chest where my heart used to be. I either needed to kill him and get it done or fix it. Loyalty to my father said to kill him, but my heart... my heart was begging me to fight for what we wanted. To fix us. I was stuck between family and love. A decision that no person should have to make.

I wanted to go to him right away after I left my father's house but I didn't want him to see me bruised and bloody from the hands of my father. So, I waited only long enough for the bruising around my throat and my eye to fade to a point they could be covered with makeup.

"How long?" I ask barging into Alessandro's house, finding him in his kitchen. Jeans slung low on his hips, a dress shirt hanging open revealing hard ridges of muscle and a smattering of dark hair on his chest.

He ignores the question, cracking open a new beer and lighting up smoke. He looks relaxed, unaffected by the fact that my family sent me to kill him because he was De Luca's, right-hand man.

"How. Long?" I ask again, my hands tightening around the blade until my knuckles turn white. I didn't want to kill him but self-preservation had me bringing my weapon of choice.

"How long have I known you were to kill me?" He leans against the kitchen counter, ankle casually crossed over the other, cigarette dangling between long fingers. Fingers that have done unimaginable things to me. I swallow hard and force those images down.

Alessandro unhurriedly brings the cigarette to his lips, slowly inhaling a drag and blowing it out toward the ceiling. "Known for a while. Have to say, I was surprised when you didn't try pushing that blade through my chest that first day you stumbled into my apartment, but then you put out so easy and I figured why not have a little fun first."

"You bastard," I seethe, charging toward him. Not realizing until his strong grip is wrapped around my wrist suspended in the air that I had raised the knife as I rushed him.

"What happened, love? You get a proper look at me and decide to climb me like a tree before doing your family's dirty work? You wanted a taste of my dick first? Got more than that, though, didn't you?" A cocky smirk pulls at his lips.

My other hand shoots up in a fist ready to pound into his chest, but he catches that one too. Spinning me around so fast, the wind gets knocked out of me when my lower back connects with the hard edge of the granite countertop. Alessandro wrenches the knife from my hand, pinning both my wrists behind my back in one of his.

"I-I never…" I try to swallow past the lump in my throat but it's no use. Tears threaten to spill but I will them back.

"You never what? Never wanted to kill me? Never wanted to fuck me? Which is it, Romanov?" His face is turning red, his eyes morphing from their usual grey to the darkest black I've ever seen, a vein pulses on his forehead. How did I royally fuck this up?

"I never wanted to kill you," I whisper, the fight draining from me. I can't do this anymore. I can't pretend that he's just another job, that he doesn't mean anything to me. "I'm so sorry, Alessandro. Please, believe me."

"No? Then why the fuck did you just charge at me with the blade pointed at my fucking chest?"

His fingers curl around the handle of the blade laying on the counter behind me, his other hand fisting the hair at the nape of my neck, tugging my head back until my throat is exposed. The edge of the blade coming to rest just above my collarbone.

I close my eyes and will my heart rate to slow. "Please, Alex," I beg. "I didn't want any of this. They made me -"

"Don't give me that bullshit, Jessika," he interrupts me, pressing the blade further into my skin. "Why should I trust anything coming out of the mouth of a Romanov anyway?"

I wince at the sharp pinch and trickle of blood from under the tip of the blade. "I-I..." I take in a deep breath, as deep as I can with a knife pressed against my throat and try again. If he's determined to kill me then he has to know the truth. I was done with the lies. "I never wanted to kill you. I begged them to leave you alone. To spare your life. They told me that either I had to do it or they would send my sister. I... I couldn't stand the thought of her..." I blow out a frustrated breath, meeting his steely eyes. "I thought if I could at least get close to you I could try and protect you for as long as I could."

That's bullshit. I know it. He knows it. Alessandro didn't need protection, especially any help from me. He can handle himself better than anyone I know.

I hold my breath, waiting for his reaction. He laughs. I just came clean about everything, with a knife pressed to my damn throat - against the fading bruises might I add- and he's laughing. Placing my hands, palms down on his chest I shove him, but he doesn't budge. Instead, his fingers tighten around my hair and I yelp at the sharp pain at the base of my skull, then tears start flowing down my cheeks with the new pressure he's putting on the blade. More blood trickles down my chest.

"I can protect myself, Angel."

I want to protest that while that's true he doesn't know my family, but then the blade's gone and his head dips, seconds before his tongue licks up the top of my breast, along my collarbone, and up my neck. His lips come down on mine moments later, his tongue running along the seam of my lips until they part for him. The metallic taste on his tongue surprises me at first but then it gives way to the taste of him I've come to love and I moan into his mouth, my hands curling into fists around his open shirt.

I hear the clink of the blade falling against the stone countertop at the same time Alessandro's hand curls around my hip, pulling me flush against him. I push him away and before I allow myself any time to think, I grab the knife from the counter holding it out in front of me. I'm surprised when my hand doesn't shake under the pressure I'm putting on the handle.

Alessandro smirks, stalking towards me. He hits the knife out of my hand but he doesn't stop advancing. His one hand curling around the nape of my neck, his lips descending on mine in a bruising kiss.

"Stop." I shove him back again not realizing my hand's moving until my palm connects with the side of his face.

But that doesn't deter him, not even for a moment. Alessandro keeps coming. This time he wraps a fist around the hair at the nape of my neck, tugging my head back, his other hand wrapping around my throat as his licks his way into my mouth. My knees go weak, threatening to give out from under me but his hips pin me against the counter, his cock twitching against my lower belly.

"I love when you fight me, Angel," he says biting down on my lower lip and I whimper from the mixture of pain from the old bruises and pleasure Alessandro's hand wrapped around my throat provides.

"I'm no Angel." I shove him off me again, watching as he barely catches himself against the breakfast bar, arms bent at the elbows, fingers curled around the edge of the stone. He looks like every woman's fantasy with that knowing grin plastered on his face.

Oh, fuck it. What would it hurt to use him one last time?

I move toward him on shaking legs, gripping his shirt in my hands and shoving it down his arms until it lays in a pool of black behind him. Alessandro pulls my shirt off, dropping it to the floor with the remnants of his dress shirt. His hands graze down my sides, around my back and continuing their way down until they curl under my ass and lift me, my legs wrapping around his waist, my hands curling around the nape of his neck as

Alessandro slams me back against the wall separating the kitchen from the living room.

"Fight me," he growls, his fingers curling around my throat.

"No," I squeak out.

"Fucking fight me," he snarls, bringing my face closer to his by my throat before slamming me back against the wall again.

I don't answer him, my fingers fumbling with the zipper on his jeans as I try to grind against him. I need to feel his skin against mine, need to feel his hard body caging me in.

"Jessika," he groans when my fingers wrap around his hard length. His breath coming in pants against the curve of my neck.

"Fuck me, Alessandro. I don't want to think. I don't want to fight. I just want to feel you moving inside me."

That seems to be all the encouragement he needs. He swats my hand away from his cock and pushes into me in one deep thrust, my body bowing off the wall from the sheer force. His hold around my throat doesn't waver, his other hand gripping my hip as he leans down to grunt in my ear.

"Is this what you want, Angel? You want me to fuck this pussy so hard that you don't know where I end and you begin? So hard that you won't be able to walk outta here?"

"Yes! God, yes!" I claw at his back, trying to hold on to something, anything to keep me anchored in this moment.

"Let go, Angel."

I try to swallow past his grip on my throat and shake my head. I don't want this to end. If I let go and allow my body to give in the orgasm threatening to wash over me then I'll be forced back into reality. I'm not ready for that yet. I want to stay in this moment with him a little longer.

"Fucking stop thinking and let go, Jessika," he grunts in my ear, frustration simmering just below the surface.

"No," I pant.

Alessandro growls, the hand gripping my hip skimming down between our bodies. His thumb finding the nub that's sure to send me over the edge. I whimper when he applies a little pressure, trying desperately to hold on, but when he pinches my clit I know it's no use. And then I'm coming. My orgasm crashing down over me and bringing with it a new onslaught of tears.

I've barely come down from my orgasm when Alessandro lowers my legs back down, instantly pulling away from me when my feet are planted firmly on the ground.

"Get out." He turns his back on me, gathering up his shirt and slipping his arms through the sleeves.

"No," I sigh, my shoulders deflating while I struggle to pull my skirt back into place.

It happens so fast I barely have time to react. My breath hitches when the cold metal of his gun presses against the sweat-slicked flesh of my forehead. I look up and straight into the barrel of his 9mm.

There's this moment when death is staring you in the face when realization dawns that the amount of money in your bank account, how much beer is in your fridge, what trending product you did or did not buy, social media… none of it matters. What matters is not telling the people in your life that you love them. What matters is that you were too scared to take a chance on something new.

And right now, my one biggest regret is not telling my father to go fuck himself when I realized that my last job was this man standing in front of me. So what if that meant my death. At least then I wouldn't have to look in the eyes of the man I love and see nothing but hurt and betrayal. Another regret is not telling Alessandro sooner. He said he knew all along that I was sent to kill him, but at least if I had come clean then maybe, just maybe, I would've had a chance with him.

"Get. Out."

My lip quivers at the coldness of his voice. Gone is the strong, badass daughter of the Russian boss. In her place is a woman who's about to lose the love of her life for good. Ignoring the gun pointed at my head, I swipe at my tears with the back of my hand. I could try to fight him, get the gun out of his hand and turn the stakes on him but I've already hurt him enough to last a lifetime so I don't. I've already told him the truth, except for one.

"I lov –"

"Don't fucking say shit you don't mean. One last chance, Jessika. Get the fuck out of my house and don't come back. I won't hesitate to put a bullet in your head next time. A Romanov is not welcome in this house."

I should heed his threat and leave because the way his body is drawn tight, his finger hovering over the trigger there's no doubt in my mind that he'll follow through on his threat. Call me stupid but I would much rather prefer it coming from him than my father.

"No," I choke out, staring him down as I move forward an inch, the barrel pressing further into my skin. "Do it, Alessandro. Pull the trigger. Put me out of my misery because I would much rather my death be at your hands than my father's."

Alessandro stares at me, slack-jawed. No doubt taken by surprise from my admission.

"Do it," I taunt him, refusing to break eye contact.

"Jessika, don't fucking tempt me right now."

"Alessandro, please," I beg, not caring how fucked up we must look right now.

Me standing in front of him in nothing but my wrinkled skirt, him with jeans slung slow on his hips, the button still undone and pointing a gun to my head while I beg him to pull the fucking trigger.

We were two fucked up, broken people who found each other at the worst possible time. He wanted to save me by forcing me to live a life without him. I wanted him to kill me because I couldn't imagine living without him.

"Goddammit, Jessika!" he roars, the barrel pressing harder into my skull, but that wasn't what caused me to wince. No, the sight of his finger pressing down on the trigger did that.

Taking a deep breath and letting it out through my parted lips, I take a second to gather myself and steel my chin.

"I love you," I whisper a split second before the sound of a gunshot sounds through the room and I jump.

Why the fuck did I jump? I'm supposed to be dead. Dead people don't jump. I slowly will my eyes to open not realizing that I had shut them at the last minute. My head is spinning and there's a ringing in my ears. When my vision clears enough, Alessandro is on his knees a few feet in front of me, the gun still clenched in a fist resting on his thigh, his head bent, shoulders heaving.

Slowly, I twist to the side to see a hole in the wall, not even two inches from where my head just was. *Fuck that was close.* I take a tentative step towards him and then another before I'm kneeling in front of him.

"You missed. Why?"

The one thing I know about Alessandro from the countless research my father had on him, is that he never misses a shot. His head is still bent, but his entire body stills.

"For the same reason why you couldn't kill me." He clears his throat and discreetly wipes at his cheeks.

"We make quite the pair, huh?"

There's a small grin on his face when he finally concedes and lifts those amazing grey eyes to look at me. God, I love his eyes. They're like nothing I've ever seen before. But there's something unsettling about the way they're trained on me right now. I try not to squirm and grab at my tank top, pulling it over my head in hopes that it hides some of the trembling in my hands.

Alessandro grips my wrist when I stand and move to start cleaning the mess around us, my body turning to stone at his touch. His eyes roam over my face and neck. I'm assuming the makeup I used to cover up the bruises has wiped away and he's seeing the still slightly purple and blue-tinged skin. Thankfully, he doesn't grill me about how I got them.

"It's time to come clean about everything, Jessika. I'm calling Braxton."

"I'm not your Angel anymore, am I?" *Translation: I'm not yours anymore, am I?*

He doesn't answer me, but the lingering hurt and betrayal in his eyes is answer enough. I'll never be his again, and that's the worst kind of torture. Knowing I had everything in the palm of my hands, and just lost it.

"Call Braxton," I choke out past the lump in my throat. "Tell him to bring Klara. I have a lot of apologizing to do," I say and then go in search of the broom and dustpan I know he keeps in the pantry, to clean up the debris caused from the bullet hitting the wall.

Chapter 16

ALESSANDRO

JESSIKA SHIFTS NERVOUSLY from her seat on the sofa when I get up to answer the door and let Braxton and Klara in. Nobody speaks while I pour us each a drink and take a seat on the chair across from Jess. Braxton and Klara exchange confused glances, but Jess refuses to look away from a spot on the wall she's found fascinating since they arrived.

When I called to invited them over I never said why. Just that it was important for him to bring Klara. I thought I'd give Jessika the responsibility of explaining this whole fucked up situation to them.

"What's all this about Alex?" Braxton questions after a long drawn out silence.

When I first called and told him that Jessika wanted to explain everything to him, he was outraged that I hadn't taken care of the threat like I said I would. The only reason that she's alive and sitting on the sofa in my living room at this very moment is that Braxton understood that my feelings for her went deeper than I ever cared to admit but not even I could save her if he didn't like what she had to say.

I clear my throat and take a healthy sip of the amber

liquid in my glass. "Jessika," I prompt.

Her shoulders round as she straightens up and looks Braxton in the eyes before her gaze swings over to Klara. "First, I want you to know that I never intended to go through with any of it..." she starts and I scoff but she continues like she never heard me. "And I never meant to put you in danger or... or to betray you."

"The only reason you're still breathing is that Alessandro asked me to hear you out, but make no mistake I will not hesitate to do what he couldn't." Braxton leans forward, elbows braced on his knees.

If I didn't hate her, I would almost admire her strength at this moment. The way she steals her chin and refuses to back down. Jessika inhales deeply, letting it out through her parted lips. "I grew up as the odd one out in my family. I never understood the things they did and the measures they went to achieve something. No child should grow up afraid of their own family, their blood. When I was twelve I made a vow to myself that I would never allow them to make me into one of them. I vowed that when I was old enough I would leave and not look back, that I would start over where nobody knew me. Where nobody knew the name of my family. And I did.

The night before my eighteenth birthday, I left and I didn't look back. When nothing happened a couple months later, I enrolled in my first year of college under a different surname, I applied for a student loan and was approved before classes started. Everything was great for that year, I was finally starting to relax into a routine, thinking that they must've given up on me or something."

Her eyes squeeze shut and I can see that she's

struggling with the memories but I refuse to comfort her. My fingers grip the arm of the chair a little harder.

"The morning of my nineteenth birthday they came for me. Ripped me out of my bed at four in the morning. The reason I know the exact time is because my alarm clock reflected the numbers on the ceiling and I remember it being the first thing I saw when that hand clamped down on my mouth."

While Jessika keeps telling them what happened next, my eyes stay glued to Klara, watching her every reaction and the moment she realizes what's happening. Why I asked them to come over.

"Your... Your family's the reason you were in that building?"

Jess swallows hard and nods, slipping her hands out of Klara's when Klara goes to take Jessika's hands in hers.

"I realized what was happening when I caught a glimpse of Dante and Gio in that first week. Dante was always kissing up to my father, ready to do whatever he asked because he was certain that father would be agreeable to join the two families when the time came for him to take over as Don. I don't think he ever thought you'd come back and claim your birthright after your father died, Braxton. But when you did, I think it enraged him to the point that he pledged his full allegiance to my father-"

"Wait," Klara interrupts turning to her fiancé. "You never wanted to be the Don?"

Braxton reaches Klara's hand, kissing the top of hers before leaning back in his seat. "I rebelled against the family a lot in my teenage years. I had been groomed to take over for as long as I can remember but that doesn't mean that I always wanted to. I spent several years doing everything I could to distance myself from La Famiglia. When my father died I knew I needed to become the man he groomed me to be," he explains then turns his attention back to Jessika. "What about Giovanni?"

"Gio was always a dirty rat who only cared about which family could pay him the most money. I-I didn't know about you, Klara. I didn't know *that* part of my father's business until…" Her voice trails off.

I'm half impressed that Braxton has managed to keep his cool - barely - through hearing this and half impressed that Jessika keeps talking. I didn't think she would actually tell them everything.

"My father was sending me a message by handing me over to those men. No matter how far I run, he'll always drag me back and won't hesitate to put me in my place. No matter how hard I fight, he'll always beat me down. When I left the hospital, he was waiting for me outside, said he had a proposition for me. If I do things for him, he'll let me have my freedom. He'll let me walk away from the family."

"What things?" Braxton questions, his jaw ticking. He already knows she was meant to kill me, but he's testing her. Wanting to know if he can really trust the words coming from her mouth.

"Do you know what a black widow is?"

"Like the spider?" Klara cocks her head to the side, but Jessika shakes her head no.

"He made you use your body to lure men before killing them."

Jessika looks over to Braxton and gives him a clipped nod before turning her gaze back to the hands in her lap.

"Jessika…" Klara gasps, covering her mouth with

the palm of her hand.

"How many?"

I gulp down the rest of my drink and go to the kitchen to pour another. The first part of her story is fucked up on so many levels. I still don't understand how her father could care so less about his daughter to pay someone to rape her repeatedly.

"Four." I hear her answer as I round the corner back into the living room and take my seat again. "I-I have one more." She glances up at me, her emerald eyes still pleading with me. "But I refuse to do it. I won't do it."

"Who is it? Who does he want you to kill?" Braxton sits up straighter.

"Me," I supply for her and the room goes silent.

"Like I said, I refuse to do it. I will not do it."

"What happens if you don't?" Klara asks the question we're all thinking.

"He'll kill me," Jessika's voice is low, defeated when she answers. "It was supposed to be done by this morning. By now my father has realized that I was serious when I told him I refused to go through with it and he'll be sending someone to take me out."

"But why?" Klara questions, her brows furrowed in confusion. "Why would your own father want to kill you? Because you refused to kill Alessandro?"

Jessika nods. "Because he can no longer control me. He trained me, broke me down and built me back up so that I would take orders from him without question. I know the ins and outs of his business. I know how his mind works and exactly where to hit to hurt him. I can single-handedly bring him down. I'm a bigger threat to him now that I have severed any loyalty I had to my family." She takes a deep breath before continuing. "Look, Braxton, you don't have to believe me. Hell, I don't think I expect you to, but I'm not a threat to you or the Famiglia."

Braxton studies her for several minutes. The air in the room growing thicker with each tick of the clock that goes by in silence. I can tell Klara wants to say something but she wisely chooses to keep her mouth shut.

Eventually, he stands pulling Klara up with him. "You're right, Jessika, you are no threat to the Famiglia, but I don't trust you."

Klara looks from Braxton to Jessika and back again. Her eyes widening in the realization of what Braxton is about to do. "Brax, no…" she starts but the slight shake of his head brokers no room for argument.

"You made your bed now you must lie in it, Jessika."

Braxton grabs Klara by the hand as he turns to leave. I should've known that she would not go willingly. Klara is a spitfire when she wants to be. She'll go to bat for people if she feels they've been wronged, even people she barely knows, and she most definitely isn't afraid to put Braxton in his place. Kind of like she's about to do now.

"Klara," he warns.

She pulls her hand out of his, cocking her hip and crossing her arms over her chest. "No, Braxton. I know you're not that completely heartless-"

"It has nothing to do with heart, Mia Bella, and everything to do with protecting this family."

"Jessika is part of that family, Braxton, whether you want to admit it or not. She became part of this family the minute Alessandro invited her for dinner."

I choke and sputter on the gulp of liquor I just took. Ignoring the way it burns as it fights its way up my nose. Klara turns to me, fire in her eyes and I wisely stop whatever protest was about to leave my mouth.

"Don't you deny it, Alex," she says, pointing a finger at me. "She's the only girl you've ever invited over for family dinner."

"It's not like that, baby girl." I hoped by using my nickname for her that she would be swayed to take my side. I should've known that women will always stick together.

"Yeah? And how many women have you told about your brother?"

I curse under my breath because she's right. The only people outside of my parents that know about my brother are the people in this room. Thanks to some hot sex and pillow talk, Jessika now knows everything there is to know about me. That just reminds me that while she knows everything about me, I know nothing about her. The woman I'm in love with is nothing but a stranger.

"That's what I thought," Klara says smirking before turning back to Braxton. "As far as I'm concerned, Jessika is family. You yourself have said that family always protects its own."

"Mia Bella, how can you be sure that this isn't some trick? That once we agree to help her, she won't turn around and twist the knife in my back?"

"*She* is right here," Jessika huffs. I can tell she's trying to put the tough girl mask back on, and while it may work on other people, I know her too intimately to know that she's trying and failing. I want to go to her, pull her into my arms and tell her that I'll do everything in my power to make sure she lives to see another day. That we'll both live to see another day, but my anger is still too close to the surface and if I get my hands on her, I can't guarantee that I won't follow through on my previous promise of killing her.

"Braxton De Luca!" Klara's hands fly to her hips as she narrows her eyes. "You saw her in that room next to mine. You saw what they did to her. Family does not do that. Family does not treat each other as if they are expendable. Her father is no more her family than Dante was yours."

"You picking her side over me, Mia Bella?" Braxton's voice lowers. It's the voice that makes grown men quiver in their shoes but doesn't seem to have an effect on Klara except to fire her up even more.

"No, Brax. *I* didn't create sides. *You* did. *I* would rather work together to find a solution that saves this family, including Jessika." Klara pauses for a breath, glancing over at Jessika with a small smile before turning back to her fiancé. When she speaks again her voice is small. "And I'll tell you something else, Braxton. If you want this wedding to move forward then you'll do everything in your power to make sure that Jessika isn't harmed."

Fuck, I knew she wasn't afraid to stand up to Braxton but never in a million years would I ever have expected those words to leave her lips. Klara loves Braxton with everything she is and if she's willing to give up her life with Braxton to save Jessika then she must see something in the Bratva princess that we don't.

"Are you threatening me, Mia Bella?"

"No. It's no threat, Braxton. It's a promise. You may not consider her family, but I do." Klara calmly collects her purse, goes over to hug Jessika and whispers something in her ear that causes a tear to slip down Jessika's cheek. Klara pulls away, smiling down at Jessika and then turns her intense gaze on me as she makes her way over. I try not to squirm in my seat. How is it possible that this little thing manages to cause this reaction out of me?

Klara wraps her arms around my waist, pressing her cheek to my chest. "You of all people shouldn't be so quick to judge, Alessandro," she whispers and I know she's talking about my brother.

She doesn't say another word when she pulls away and stomps past Braxton, not giving him the satisfaction of an acknowledgment as she pushes past him and out my front door. Braxton exhales loudly, running a hand through his dark hair. Then the sound of a car starting up penetrates the silence in the house. Braxton's head snaps up, his ears trained on the sound.

I drop my chin to my chest to try and hide the smirk threatening to split across my face because I recognize the sound of the car and have a pretty good feeling what's about to happen next. I'm already pulling my keys out of my pocket when Braxton curses moving towards the front door.

"For fuck's sake. Klara!" Braxton comes back in the room, eyes wild, fists clenching. My keys are already sailing through the air toward him before he can ask.

"Don't reck it," I yell after him as he rushes out the door to go after his girl.

Klara never fails to amaze me. She keeps Braxton on his feet, and nothing she ever does is ever predictable.

"Are they always like that?" Jessika asks from her seat on the sofa.

"Almost since day one."

"Are they going to be okay?" Jessika looks nervous when she looks over her shoulder out the window to the driveway where Klara and Braxton just peeled out of.

"They'll be fine."

The air is thick with awkward tension, neither one of us quite knowing what to say to the other. Jessika sighs, running her palms down the front of her pants before standing.

"Well, I guess I'll go then."

Stay seated, Alessandro. Let her go. She's no longer your responsibility.

Jessika hasn't taken five steps before I'm moving, gripping her bicep and halting her progress towards the door, but as soon as she turns around, I drop my hand.

"Stay." I cross my arms over my chest to prevent myself from reaching for her again. "At least until we know what's happening next. You can take the guest room."

Jessika takes a step closer and another and another until there's less than an inch separating us, her small hands coming up to rest palm down on my chest. My cock twitches behind the zipper of my jeans. I might be furious with her, but he doesn't give a damn.

"Jessika," I warn between clenched teeth, trying not to breath in the intoxicating scent of the vixen in front of me.

"Please, Alessandro. I said I was sorry."

If this was anyone else, I would already be balls deep, fucking out the anger and frustration coursing through my veins. But it's not anyone else. It's Jessika. And for once I don't feel like getting naked regardless of the state of my dick. She betrayed me and I don't think I can ever forgive her for that.

I take a step back, causing her hands to fall away and ignore the flash of hurt and tears welling up in her eyes.

"Guest room is up the stairs and to the right. I'll be back later."

"Where are you going?" she calls after my retreating back, her breath hitching with each sob.

And because things aren't fucked up enough as it is, I find myself replying before I can clamp my mouth shut. "To find someone to fuck."

The last thing I hear before the garage door shuts behind me is Jessika shocked gasp. I'm going to hell. On a one-way ticket. Do not pass go, do not collect two-hundred dollars.

***
JESSIKA

The sounds of the garage door rolling up and a motorcycle revving are deafening in the now empty house.

To find someone to fuck.

He wouldn't. He couldn't possibly already be able to move on from what we had so soon. It hadn't even been more than two hours since I was the one he was taking up against the wall in his kitchen. But then what did I expect? I lied to him. Betrayed his trust. What did I think was going to happen? That Alessandro would somehow be able to accept my betrayal and still take me to bed and make love to me like before?

I go through the motions of walking up the stairs and locating the guest bedroom, but my mind isn't on my actions. It's on Alessandro and the faceless person that will be sharing his bed tonight when it should be me.

You fucked up your chances, Jess. Live with it.

I don't bother stripping out of my clothes or pulling back the sheets on the bed, choosing instead to curl up in a ball on top of the covers and let the tears flow freely.

Chapter 17

ALESSANDRO

THE LIGHTS OF the club are too bright. The music too loud, but the glass of whiskey between my fingers is exactly what I need to forget the last week ever happened. Well, step one at least. Step two would be finding a warm welcoming hole to stick my cock for the night.

After jumping on my motorcycle and leaving Jessika behind at my house I didn't have a clue where I was headed. All I knew was that I needed to get away and I needed to go fast. Next thing I know, I'm pulling up outside a gay club in the next town over.

Now I'm sitting in a darkened corner of the bar and wondering how the fuck I managed to make things worse, and they were worse. I knew that once I left the house things would never be the same with Jessika, especially after the words I said before I left.

Klara was right. I laid everything out there for Jessika about what I did to my brother when we were kids. I didn't leave out any details. She knew I had killed my brother in cold blood and yet she still stayed. She stayed and she never once looked at me like I was monster. I never understood why at first because a monster was what I was. A monster was what I would be again if I ever let the firm grip on my control and anger slip. But she saw me, all of me, and she still uttered those three words.

I love you.

She could've turned her back on me, continued to carry out her father's demands that she kill me after learning what I was capable of, but she didn't. And yet, when she needed me the most, I turned my back on her.

She was willing to defy her father, defy the Bratva for me. She was willing to lay down her life in exchange for mine. And I was the asshole that just walked away.

I slam the rest of my drink back and move to retrieve my wallet from the back pocket of my jeans to pay my tab ready to get back to the house. That's when something in me tells me to look across the bar, but all I see is the silhouette of a man sitting on the other side of the bar. He's fully encased in the shadows but that doesn't stop my curiosity or lesson the way an invisible string pulls tight, urging me to go to him. My dick is also standing up and taking notice of this complete stranger before we've even seen him. My feet start moving without my command, carrying me closer until I'm standing directly in front of him. He leans back against the bar, elbows resting on the hard surface, spreading his legs in invitation and I step between them without further coaxing. That's when I get my first good look at him and realize why I would be so drawn to him. The way he looks up at me from under dark lashes, biting his lip, his eyes perusing my body but never touching me, it does something to me that I haven't been able to find with Jessika.

In order to do my job successfully I've had to

become good at reading people especially when my job entails making deals with drug dealers, motorcycle clubs, trading guns and other firearms. Lives are constantly on the line and if I make even one mistake, the life lost could belong to a member of the Famiglia.

From looking at this man I can tell he won't fight me like Jessika does, he'll do what I say because I said, and he may on occasion want to top from the bottom, he'd gladly let me fuck him six ways from Sunday.

He's the light to Jessika's dark.

Sun-bleached blond hair falls over one eye, I'm tempted to push it back off his face so that there's no barrier between me and his blue eyes. Square cut jaw, a chin dimple that I'm itching to lick while I pound into his tight ass. Blondie pushes up from the bar stool, his body brushing up against mine as he straightens to his full height. He's tall, maybe only a couple inches shorter than my six-six.

Images of him fucking Jessika's ass while I pound into her pussy assault me and I groan, punching my hips forward into his. Our dicks rubbing up against each other through the fabric of our jeans.

Blondie hooks a finger in a belt loop of my pants and moves around me, successfully pulling me along behind him down the hall and past the bathrooms. He turns, pushing me up against a wall in the dark corner, his fingers digging into my hips as his raises his lips and captures mine in a searing kiss.

I've always been the one in control. I don't bottom. Ever. But Christ, this is hot, and I'll gladly give him the illusion of being in control... for now. Blondie licks his way into my mouth, and with a groan I open for him, sucking his tongue into my mouth as he expertly undoes the button and zipper on my jeans, then reaches in to wrap a calloused hand around my throbbing cock.

"Fuck," I growl, throwing my head back until it hits the wall with a dull thud.

He licks up my neck, nipping at my earlobe before falling to his knees and wrapping those perfect bow lips around the head of my cock. I'm about two seconds from gripping the back of his head in my hands and fucking his mouth.

Blondie bops up and down on my length, hollowing out his cheeks and increasing the suction after every pass. Then he takes my entire length down his throat and swallows. I groan low and long as the telltale tingle works its way up my spine after a few more expert licks.

"Shit. Going to come," I warn, but that just makes him repeat the motion again and again until my balls tighten and draw up, and I'm spilling down his throat.

He looks up at me with heavy-lidded eyes and licks the head of my cock clean before running his tongue along the seam of his lips and standing. I grab him by the sides of his face and haul him to me, my mouth slamming down on his in a bruising kiss. I can taste myself on his tongue and it's the most erotic thing I've ever tasted. I've tasted myself on Jessika, but it's different tasting it on another man.

Jessika.

Fuck. Fuck. Fuck.

What was wrong with me? Was I that much of an asshole that I completely forgot about the woman who holds my fucking heart? The woman I left alone in my house and hurting.

"Let's get out of here," Blondie whispers, his warm breath against my ear sending shivers down my body.

Here's where I'm supposed to push him away, tell him thanks but no thanks because I have a girl, but I don't. I pull him into another kiss, this time I take my time exploring his mouth making sure that he knows exactly who's in control. When I pull back, his lips are swollen and his eyes are half-lidded. Fuck, he's beautiful, but I won't fuck him here… like this. When I fuck him and make no mistake I *will* fuck him, it'll be with Jessika watching.

"Give me your phone."

"What?" he asks, stunned.

"Phone. Now."

Like a good little boy, he reaches into the back pocket of his jeans and places the smartphone in my outstretched palm. I find his contacts and add my name and cell number as well as a location.

"What's your name, Blondie?"

"K-Kase," he says shifting from foot to foot, looking back down the hall like he's worried we'll be caught.

I send myself a text so that I have his name and number before handing the phone back to him. When he reaches out to take back the phone, I wrap a hand around his wrist and pull him flush against my chest, my cock already hardening again, and kiss him one last time. Unlike the other kisses we've exchanged tonight, this one offers a promise of more to come.

When we finally come up for air his cheeks are flushed, lips even more swollen and probably a little bruised, eyes glazed over. I have to force myself to move away from him or I'll do something I'll regret. Like, take him up against the wall in this dingy club… without Jessika. Before making my way back down the hallway I issue one last demand, a well of satisfaction bubbling up when Kase's cheeks flush hotter and he nods.

"That location. Tomorrow night at eight."

***
JESSIKA

I didn't hear Alessandro come home the night before, but that doesn't really surprise me. After my head hit the pillow and I was all cried out, sleep took me over and I stayed asleep the rest of the night until bright sunlight streamed through the open curtains of the guest room.

When I pad downstairs I'm half expecting Alessandro to not be there and half expecting him to be there with someone else, which is why I'm surprised when I round the corner into the kitchen to find him standing in front of the coffee maker by himself. Loose fitting sweatpants hang from his hips, and when he turns there's no mistaking the outline of his thick cock. I begin moving towards him only to be halted mid-stride by his comment from last night.

To find someone to fuck.

Someone to fuck...

I swallow hard past the lump in my throat as I'm overcome by so many questions. How long was he out last night? Where did he go? Did he find someone to fuck? And if he did, did he bring them here? Did he spend the night at their place and just get back early this morning?

"I can hear you thinking from here, Angel," he says, lifting the coffee mug to his lips. Lips that swollen.

My stomach drops and I have to grip the edge of the counter to keep myself up. Tears begin to well up in my eyes but I will them down. I am not weak dammit!

"Don't call me that," I bite out. "Did you find

someone else to fuck, Alessandro?"

Alessandro watches me over the rim of his coffee mug then he calmly places the mug in the sink, turning around to face me and leaning back against the counter like he hasn't a care in the world. I'm not sure I even want to know the answer to that question but when I look up into his grey eyes I know.

"You fucking asshole!" I hiss.

Alessandro stalks towards me, grabbing me by the wrists and pinning me against his solid chest when I try to push him away. "Stop it, Jessika."

"Was it good? Was her pussy tighter than mine? Did she fight you like you like, Alessandro? Did she?" I scream in his face, trying my hardest to wrench my wrists free and punch his chest but when his grip tightens I know there's no use.

"*He* sucked cock just fine."

"Go fuck your-" the rest of the words die on my tongue when what he just said sinks in. I should muster up every last bit of strength I have and push him away, run upstairs, gather my shit and leave. I should demand to know why. Why would he do that to us?

Us?

There is no longer an *us*. We stopped existing as a couple the minute the truth was revealed, but the thought of him with someone else so soon after should hurt. It should cut deep. Then why does it turn me on knowing that another man sucked him off? That his tongue was down another man's throat? If it was any other woman, I would've demanded to know her name and I would go cut a bitch. How is the fact that it wasn't another woman but a man make me less rage-y and more horny?

Alessandro chuckles when my face heats to a

flaming red. My tongue darting out to lick along my bottom lip.

"We have a lot to talk about before he arrives tonight. Grab a coffee and something to eat, Angel, we'll talk when you're done."

"Wait, you invited him back here? Tonight?"

"Si. Wanted to fuck him in that club last night…"

I shove away from him and back away but Alessandro doesn't allow me to go far before he's pulling me back against him. His fingers fisting the hair at the nape of my neck and tugging until I'm forced to look up at him.

"I wanted you to be there, Angel. I want you to watch while I fuck him and then we're both going to fuck you."

My breaths start coming in heavy pants as Alessandro continues talking, my thighs pressing together.

"Do you want that, Angel? A cock in each hole. Filling you up and fucking you so hard you'll have a hard time walking tomorrow. And every time you sit, you'll be forced to remember the way his cock felt in your tight ass while I fucked your tight pussy."

"Yes," I moan, melting into him.

"Good," he says pulling away. "Now eat breakfast and then we'll talk." He slaps my ass on his way out the kitchen.

Jesus, this man is hell on my heart… and my body.

I scarf down a toasted bagel and coffee, then go in search of Alessandro wanting to know more about his plan for tonight. I find him in his office and have to take a minute to just admire him. Alessandro is standing by the window, his back to me. I still can't get over how built this man is, if I didn't know any better I would think he was a professional wrestler or bodybuilder. My fingers itch to explore every dip and ridge of rippling muscle across his back, down to the twin dimples on his lower back.

I always thought I'd end up with a man who was covered head to toe in tattoos. I had visions of licking each and every line of the intricate artwork, but Alessandro... a tattoo machine has never touched his beautiful skin and I wouldn't have it any other way. His muscles more than make up for things to run my tongue along.

"Are you going to come in or do you plan on staring at my back all day?" The deep timbre of his voice washes over me sending goosebumps scattering over my skin.

"Just taking in the view," I say, moving in behind him, tentatively placing my hands on his back while kissing his shoulder.

"And is it to your liking?"

"Very much so." I place another kiss on his opposite shoulder all the while skimming the tips of my fingers down his back and around to his hips.

Alessandro turns, framing my face between his palms. "If tonight isn't what you want, tell me and I'll put a stop to it."

"But this is your fantasy, isn't it? To watch another man fuck me before you both fill my holes?"

"Christ, Jessika," Alessandro hisses, leaning his forehead against mine. "It might be my fantasy, baby, but you're more important to me. Tell me no and it stops. Fantasy be damned."

"I-I want to try," I say, closing my eyes when Alessandro presses a soft kiss to my forehead.

"Let's go have a bath, Angel, then I'm going to make

sure that the only person you think about while he's in this tight ass is me."

"Are we going to talk more about my family?" I ask.

"Later."

***

The doorbell rings and I'm instantly on edge. I'm not sure what to expect from tonight. I mean, I want this. Being double penetrated has always been something I've fantasized about, but more than that I want to give Alessandro this. I want to show him that this relationship is more than what it started out as. What better way to do that than to give a part of myself no one else has had to him.

Deep voices echo from the front door downstairs and then heavy footsteps grow louder the closer they get to the top of the staircase and the door of Alessandro's bedroom. I swallow hard when the door handle twists and pushes open, wiping my sweaty palms on the sheer black fabric of the new lingerie I bought with Mel. It leaves absolutely nothing to the imagination but it makes me feel sexy and right now that's all that matters.

My breath hitches in my throat when Alessandro walks through the door, followed by a man that belongs on the cover of a surf magazine. His hair is bleach blond, but I'm assuming it's more from the amount of time he spends outdoors in the sun than from a bottle and falls slightly over his blue sapphire eyes. I have never seen eyes such a dark blue on a person before, but when our eyes lock they blaze and morph into black.

"This is Kase," Alessandro whispers against my ear

from behind me, his finger trailing down my arms but his eyes never leaving Kase.

"Hello, Kase," my voice is a breathless whisper but must have been loud enough for him to hear.

He closes the distance between us, hands flying to my waist where his thumbs rub small circles against my belly. "Hello, Jessika." His voice is deep, not as deep as Alessandro's, but enough to cause a shiver to race down my body.

Kase flexes his fingers against my hips and then he's spinning me around to face Alessandro, my back to Kase's front. His breath whisper-soft against my neck and shoulder, following the trail of his fingers as they slip under the thin spaghetti straps of the lingerie and slide down my arms. The flimsy, black material pooling at my feet.

Kase's lips kissing down my spine sends a new round of shivers up my body, and when he reaches my lower body, running his tongue along the dip where my ass meets my lower back, I still for a second before Alessandro's touch relaxes me again.

Alessandro tips my chin up and kisses me while Kase continues his exploration of my body from the back. "Part your legs for him, Angel," Alessandro instructs between kisses, his hands massaging my swollen breasts.

I widen my stance enough for Kase's fingers to explore my slit. I moan into Alessandro's mouth and feel him grin against my lips, his fingers sliding down my belly to join Kase's on my clit. My hips buck, chasing the friction the two of them are creating. Then Kase slides a finger into my wet heat while his tongue licks up my crack. He nips at my skin before licking me again. Alessandro's fingers continue their dance on my clit, rubbing, pinching, driving me fucking wild. I can't take it anymore. I need more.

I grab at Alessandro's shirt, pushing it up his hard torso and until he pulls it off when my fingertips can no longer reach high enough, his belt and his jeans are the next to go. I freaking love when he goes commando. Kase's finger and tongue momentarily leave my body but then they're back after a shirt lands at my feet in my periphery.

"Bend over at your knees, Angel, show Kase that pretty ass," Alessandro groans when my hand wraps around his thick length.

I do as I'm told. My new position puts my mouth at the perfect level to suck Alessandro's cock. I grip his base and lick up his length, sucking the head of his cock into my mouth. I moan when Kase parts my ass cheeks and licks around the puckered hole. Alessandro hisses, bucking his hips and thrusting his cock deeper down my throat.

Soon the pads of Kase's fingers are replacing his tongue, I still, even as every fiber of my being is on fire from his touch. Alessandro reaches down and pinches my nipples, drawing another moan from deep in my throat, he groans when my throat tightens around his length. Kase slips a finger past the tight ring of muscle in my ass. It hurts and feels weird at first but Alessandro's touch helps me relax enough to let Kase in further and the pain slowly starts to fade to a delicious burn.

Alessandro grips the back of my head, pulling me off him. "Enough. When I come it'll be in that pussy or his ass, but not this mouth of yours," he says, his thumb running along my bottom lip.

Alessandro glances over my shoulder, nodding to

Kase in a silent communication, and then he's lying on his back in the middle of the bed, his cock standing proudly at attention. "Get over here and ride me, Angel."

With a little nudge from Kase, I move towards Alessandro, the bed dipping under the weight of one knee and then another until I'm crawling over him, positioning myself above the head of his cock. Alessandro grips my hips, and I slide down, taking his entire length inside of me at once. I hear the sound of a foil wrapper tearing in the distance then Kase is behind me again, his lips kissing and nipping up my shoulder and along my neck, his finger slipping between Alessandro and me to find my clit. My head drops back against his shoulder as he rubs my clit while I ride Alessandro.

A hand wraps around the hair at the nape of my neck, pushing me forward until I'm bent over Alessandro. His lips searching out my own in a kiss. I whimper when cold liquid runs down the crack of my ass to the puckered hole. Then Kase's face is so close to mine, but it's not my mouth he's seeking out. Unbridled lust burns behind his eyes when he locks gazes with Alessandro and pulls him up by the nape of his neck for a kiss.

I'm so turned on from watching them kiss, my pussy tightens around Alessandro making him groan and buck up harder. Kase bites Alessandro bottom lip, pulling it between his teeth and then letting it go. Alessandro's nostrils flare, his hand snaking around the back of Kase's head and pulls him down to him in a bruising kiss. That's when I feel the head of Kase's cock nudging my back entrance.

I was beginning to think I was just a spectator in this

threesome, but oh boy, was I wrong because then they both turn their hungry gazes to me. Kase wraps his fist in my hair, tugging my head back as he slides deeper. Alessandro's thumb rub continues circles on my clit and when Kase finally slides all the way home I don't think I've ever felt this full. I mean, it's not my first time trying anal but it is the first time that I've been filled in both holes.

"He might be fucking you too, Angel," Alessandro growls in my ear, "but this," – he thrusts hard- "this pussy is mine. You hear me? *Mine*."

"Y-Yours," I pant.

Kase growls, shoving me forward until my face is buried in Alessandro's neck. Kase's hands grip my waist while Alessandro's grip my hips and then I think dying might be an actual possibility because they both start fucking me harder. Faster. Then the dam breaks and a full body shudder washes over me from my orgasm.

Then in only a move Hulk would be capable of, Alessandro wraps his arms around both me and Kase and flips us over so that Kase is now the one on his back and I'm riding his cock reverse cowgirl style. Alessandro quickly slides a condom down his thick length and with barely any preparation, slides into Kase. I know the second he does too because Kase's grip on my waist tightens and he bites down on my shoulder. He licks away the sting when Alessandro is fully seated in his ass.

Alessandro tugs my head back and devours my mouth while never breaking his rhythm of fucking into Kase's ass. Kase curses, his cock swelling inside of me before I feel his cum filling the condom. Alessandro's thrusts falter and then he's coming with a roar, his nose buried in the crook of my neck.

"Holy shit," I pant, collapsing back onto Kase's chest, not caring that we're both sweaty. They both laugh, but I'm not so sure I could move right now even if I wanted to. My limps feel like jelly. I wince when Kase slips out of my ass. Both him and Alessandro slip out of the bed to remove and dispose of the condoms before coming back to the bed. Caging me in between their big bodies.

"We are definitely doing that again," I breathe against Alessandro's chest. "Just as soon as I can feel my limps again."

Alessandro growls and Kase laughs but I can feel the signs of another hard-on against my ass. I don't plan on us making a habit of inviting Kase into our bed, but since he's already here and this was Alessandro's fantasy, we might as well make the best of the night while we can because once Kase leaves I doubt I'll be so willing to invite him back. Not that we didn't have fun, I know I at least did and it sure as hell sounded like Alessandro enjoyed it too, but because tonight has made me realize that I don't share very well. Sure, it was hot as fuck watching them make out and then hearing Alessandro fuck Kase, but I didn't like the way my heart seized in my chest and the way the little green monster was too close to rearing its ugly head. I'd be much happier keeping Alessandro to myself.

"How you doing, Angel?" Alessandro asks, running his fingers up and down my arm while we lay in bed after Kase has just left.

I bite my lip, wondering just how much I should tell him about my previous thoughts. But if we're planning on being together then I should probably tell him the truth, right? Ugh, why is this relationship shit so hard. When I was still single, I would've chalked it up to a great night. No guilt. No little green monster of jealousy. Alessandro shifts, trying to get a better look at my face but I burrow closer into him, hiding my face in his chest because I'm afraid of the truth he'll see there.

"I'm okay," I say.

"Jessika," he growls in warning and I sigh.

"I had fun tonight. I did…"

"But?"

"But… I don't think I'm okay with sharing you again. I like what we have, Alessandro, I don't need to add someone else." I hold my breath in anticipation of his reply.

"Me too, Angel."

I lean up, looking down at him in shock. He cups my face in his palm, his thumb running over my bottom lip.

"It was fun, and it may have been one of my fantasies but this… laying here with you in my arms. I'd rather have this fantasy."

And I melt in a puddle of swoony goo. Damn, this man just gets better and better.

"So we agree? It's just you and me from here on out?" I ask.

"You and me against the world, Angel," he says pulling me in for a kiss and I roll my eyes. So cheesy, but so mine.

Chapter 18

AFTER OUR THREESOME with Kase, Alessandro and I came back to my place so that I could change and grab an overnight bag, but then one thing led to another like it always does with us and we never did make it back to his house.

I had my chance to stew yesterday, Alessandro said last night with Kase was his way of putting his past behind him and moving forward in his future with me. But looking down at the man I love while he sleeps soundly beside me, I know that nothing will ever be the same between us. Not while my sister and father are still out there. If I have any chance of keeping whatever this is with Alessandro then I need to act fast.

If I go through with my plan there's a good chance I won't be walking away. If I go through with it, there's no guarantee that Alessandro will still be mine a week, month, or even a year from now, but that doesn't make what I have to do any less important. But if I don't go through with it then there's a big guarantee that I'll always be looking over my shoulder, waiting... wondering when my sister will show up to put a bullet through our heads, or if my father will send one of his soldiers. There's no doubt in my mind that he won't be the one pulling the trigger himself. My father might be the big, bad boss of the Bratva but he'll never be caught dead killing his own flesh and blood. No, he'd rather contract it out while he sits in his fancy office.

With all the skill I've mastered over the years, I quietly slip out from under Alessandro's arm and swipe my duffel bag from its hiding spot under my side of the bed. I gingerly make my way over to the bathroom, avoiding all the areas of the floor that creak and silently pray that the light spilling out from under the bathroom door doesn't wake him.

Once I've donned my usual uniform of tight black leggings, black tank top, and zip-up hoodie, throwing my hair up in a ballerina bun atop my head I double check the contents left in the black duffel bag. Combat knives, several handguns and silencers, extra ammunition, gloves, and my black combat boots stare up at me. I don't want to chance waking Alessandro up so I'll slip on the boots once I'm out in the hall and heading for the elevator.

I make sure to turn off the bathroom light before I open the door and tiptoes passed a softly snoring Alessandro. I'm almost to the door when a thought occurs to me. Pivoting on my sock covered feet, I pad over to the kitchen and the notepad I usually keep on the island. I jot down a quick note for him, all the while looking over to the bedroom door, straining to hear any movement. Once I'm done, I quickly tack the note to the fridge and haul ass out of the apartment. Once the door quietly closed behind me, I take off for the elevator, slipping my feet in the combat boots while it descends to the underground parking garage.

Tonight is step one of taking my life back, and if I survive, step two will be exacting revenge on daddy dearest.

***

I find my sister exactly where I figured she would be. Ever since Dante was killed at the hands of Braxton De Luca, Amanda has spent every free minute here when she's not carrying out father's orders. I'm quite happy to see the place is already empty. Club goers and staff have all gone home for the night, leaving my dear older sister sitting by herself at the bar. The only things to keep her company, a shot glass and a bottle of tequila, and not the good kind either. Seems like Amanda was already punishing herself with bottom shelf alcohol.

"Hello, sister," I greet her the same way she greeted me on the phone that day. Stepping out of the shadows, the cold hard metal of the gun at my back offers the exact amount of reassurance I need to see this night through.

Amanda laughs. It's dark, the kind of laugh someone gives when they subconsciously know that this is their end. That there's no escaping their demons this time.

"Was wondering when you were going to come for me," she says after taking a shot.

"Well, wonder no more." I lean over the bar to grab another shot glass, keeping her in my periphery the entire time. I pour myself a shot of the tequila, wincing when it burns like a motherfucker, missing the smoothness that comes from a top shelf, higher quality alcohol.

The shot probably wasn't the greatest idea, but I figure it can't hurt to share a drink with my sister before I kill her. Plus, the warmth starting to sweep through my body isn't so bad.

"Did you ever think we'd end up here? About to fight for our lives… literally," she asks, nursing another shot, her dark hair falling like a blanket over her shoulder.

"Honestly? No, I didn't," I sigh, turning to look at the glass wall behind the bar. Bottles of all shapes, sizes, and colors decorate the shelf. "I never wanted this, Manda, any of it." I decide to lay it all out there since it seems like she wants to have a sisterly heart to heart before we get down to business, and it's the least I can give her.

"You always were the good one. Perfect little Jessika could do no wrong in father's eyes. You were his prize, his trophy, his perfect weapon."

Okay, not where I thought this was going but I can't say I'm surprised. I've known what Amanda thinks me ever since we were teenagers.

"And yet you never wanted in on the business," she continues. "All you ever wanted was to live happily ever after with some guy, in a house with a white picket fence." She sneers at the last part.

"What's so wrong with that? I wanted a normal life, Amanda. One where guns and blood and fighting and death isn't a part of everyday life."

"Normal will never exist for us, Jessika. We're Romanov's, we don't get the normal life. Death will always be at our back door. It doesn't matter how far you run. You can even hide, but it'll always be there. Always. You may have changed your last name but you will always have Romanov blood running through your veins. Our identity is our curse."

Amanda takes another shot and then another before continuing. I've lost track of our much alcohol she's actually consumed while I've been sitting here but if she keeps going this way then she'll be making my job a hell of a lot easier. Heck, I'm not complaining.

"And if you think your life is going to get any easier by renouncing the Bratva and the Romanov name and shagging up with Ferrara then you are sorely mistaken. You can't leave the Russian mafia for the Italians, Jessika. That's not how this works. It'll paint a bigger target on your back... on all of their backs. You think you'll be safe with the Italians?" She looks at me over her shoulder, her eyes glossy and sad. "Baby sister, you'll never be safe. You'll never be free."

I push up from my seat and away from the bar. I've had enough of this conversation. My hands are tingling, begging for me to hit something... anything. I came here for a fight and dammit I'm going to get one.

"That's where you're wrong, sister. From here on out, I make my own decisions. I'll live my life the way I want to live it, and god help anyone who tries to tell me otherwise... including our father."

Amanda laughs but doesn't say anything, and that's when I hear it. Footsteps emerging from different corners around the club and then four of our father's soldiers are surrounding us, blocking each one of my exits. So much for this being quick, but at least I'll get my fight after all.

"You knew I was coming all along." It's not a question.

Amanda stands gracefully from her seat at the bar, and if I hadn't just seen her throwback shot after shot of tequila, I would think she was perfectly sober.

"Of course, I knew. I know everything there is to know about you, dear sister. I know when you leave the apartment, where you go, how many times that Hulk of a man fucks you, I know where he lives. I. Know.

Everything," she sneers. "I also know that you're going to die here… tonight, and for once you won't be daddy's little perfect princess."

Sisters. Gotta love 'em. Even in all their jealousy.

"You're mighty sure of yourself, sister," I taunt, even while keeping track of each man as they move closer.

This is usually where people start to worry that maybe they won't make it out alive, but here's the thing… the only person in this room who stands a chance of taking me out is my sister. Why? Because our training exceeds the training the soldiers have gone through. They're expendable to our father. There will always be some tough guy who thinks he has what it takes to work for the Bratva. These guys think they're hot shit because they carry a gun, work for the Bratva, and can maybe throw a decent punch. It's almost laughable. Whereas, father insisted that we learn a variety of fighting techniques; Krav Maga, Jujitsu, Martial Arts, you name it and I've trained in them.

A slow, sly grin pulls at her lips and then she dips her chin in a slight nod, which I'm assuming was the signal the men were looking for when they all rush me at once. One of them comes at me with a swinging right hook but I block it, driving my palm up and into his chin, snapping his head back before grabbing around the back of his neck with and ending it with a knee to the face. No sooner have I pushed my knife through his chest and stood up does another grab me by my throat, the momentum pushing me back. Twisting my body, I bring my elbow down on his arms, forcing him to break the contact and allowing me time to get a knee up. The sickening sound of bone-crushing echoing around the club as he falls back, holding his bloody nose. A bullet between his eyes ends his pain. The next two are harder, father must have trained them well or they had prior training before signing their lives away to the Bratva. One even manages to get a couple hits in and I know my ribs will be screaming in pain tomorrow, but that's tomorrow. Right now, I need to focus on ending this. It's gone on long enough.

The fighting goes on for several more minutes before all four men are lying lifeless on the stone floor of the club. The life has barely left the last man's eyes when I feel the cold metal against my temple. Memories of Alessandro standing on the other side of the gun flash before my eyes but I will them away.

"Well that was disappointing," she says, not caring that the men who were supposed to protect her are lying dead on the club floor. "I was hoping there'd be more blood, more screaming. You know... the usual begging for your life bullshit."

I gingerly straighten up to my full height, one arm wrapped around my bruised ribs, the other still holding the gun at my side. She's delusional if she thinks I'm giving up my gun.

"Drop the gun, sister."

"No," I seethe, trying not to wince at the pain in my ribs.

"Drop the gun, Jess, and I'll make this as quick and painless as possible."

"Fuck you," I snarl, bringing my gun up and pointing it at her head. If I'm going down, I'm taking her with. Nothing says sisterly bonding than going to hell together.

The squeak of the front door opening and heavy footsteps bounding down the stairs is enough for Amanda to lower her guard and her gun for a second, and give me the opening I need to put a bullet through her chest. Her mouth falls open, eyes rounding in confusion and then shock as she glances down at the blood-soaked front of her shirt.

"Jessika!" I turn towards the sound of his voice and running footsteps, momentarily forgetting about my sister and then Alessandro comes into view, but he doesn't immediately run towards me, he pulls up short, hand going behind his back and pulling out his gun.

My brows furrow in confusion when I hear the sound of a gun being fired but Alessandro hadn't had time to aim, and that's when I know that for once in our lives, Amanda and I's thoughts were on the same page. I was never going to allow Amanda to walk out of this club alive, and she was never intending to go down alone.

I fall to my knees, my body suddenly too heavy for me to keep standing. Alessandro rushes toward me, catching me in his arms before I have a chance to faceplant on the cold floor. I hear another set of footsteps walking around the room, probably checking to make sure my sister and her minions are actually dead.

I want to tell Alessandro that I love him. That it was never a question of loyalty to my family versus loyalty to him because I would choose him over my family. I would always choose him. But the words don't come out, and the last thing I see before everything goes black are storm-colored eyes staring down at me.

Chapter 19

ALESSANDRO

"**WAKE UP, BABY.** Please wake up." I cradle her head in my arms, praying that if there ever was a God that he'll hear my pleading and spare her life, but the amount of blood pouring from the wound in her chest has dread flooding my veins.

"Alessandro, you need to let go so that they can help her." Braxton places a reassuring hand on my shoulder as the paramedics try to work around me. A lot of the city is on the Famiglia's payroll, including but not limited to paramedics, and the local police department. So it doesn't surprise me that as soon as I hung up with him, he called in for a medic.

I woke up to find Jessika gone and her little goodbye note on the fridge and I knew instantly that she had gone to confront her sister.

I refuse to move from my spot behind her. The logical part of my brain says that it'll be easier for them to help her if I let her go, but I can't. Last night I had come to the conclusion that I could never let Jessika go. The knowledge that she was sent by her father to kill me couldn't keep me from her. Did it make me want to punish her when I found out? Fuck yeah. I wanted to hurt her, to make her bleed, but I also wanted to keep her and claim her as mine. And maybe that was too caveman of me but I'll always feel that way about Jess. She was made for me. We were both fucked up, both came from messed up pasts, both enjoyed the high of pain. She was the Harley Quinn to my Joker. She was mine. She'll always be mine.

The two paramedics accept that they can't get me to leave her so they allow me to help by making sure her neck is straight and doesn't move while they load her up onto the board and snap a neck brace on her. I told them she didn't need one, I caught her before she could take a nose dive but it was a precaution they had to follow, and who was I to argue. I wasn't going to be the reason she was caused any more injuries.

I don't stop to talk to Braxton or Stefan as I follow them out of the building and to the waiting ambulance. I know there'll be a Famiglia meeting in my near future to discuss what went down tonight and how the fuck none of us knew that Amanda, Braxton's ex-fiancée, was Jessika's sister. I'd be asking Jessika that same question as soon as she woke up and I knew that she was going to be okay. She conveniently left out that little piece of information when she came clean to Braxton and Klara at my house a couple days ago.

Fuck, was that only just a couple days ago? It feels like more time has passed since then.

As soon as we get to the hospital's emergency entrance, the paramedics rush her through but we're told we have to wait behind in the waiting room. I want to argue with them that I'm not leaving her side for even a second, that right now I can care less about their policies. That's my woman on that stretcher. My heart.

Christ, I loved that woman and I was going to make sure I spent the rest of my life telling her just how much.

Antonio's hand on my arm prevents me from saying fuck you to everyone and following the paramedics through the double doors. When did he even get here? I don't remember him being at the club, but then again I wasn't aware of a whole lot. I heard gunshots as soon as we pried open the heavy door of the club, then I was hauling ass down the stairs only to come face to face with Jessika doubled over, Amanda bruised and blooding behind her and with a gun pointed right at Jess's back.

My world stopped right then. Everything came to a screeching halt when Amanda raised her hand and pulled the trigger that sent a bullet flying through Jessika's back and sent her to her knees.

The bitch didn't stand a chance after that because I put her down fast and had barely made it over to catch Jessika before she took a nose dive on the floor. If it was up to me, I'd bring Amanda back and then made sure she died a slow, painful death for hurting what's mine.

We've been in the waiting for over an hour when Klara comes rushing through the automated doors with Braxton and Stefan right behind her. When she sees me, she throws herself at me, wrapping her arms around my waist in a hug. Before Klara came into Braxton's life, I hated people touching me. But she's grown on me and has become like a little sister. She can definitely be annoying as fuck as a little sister, especially if she's bugging me about something – like my dating life over the last two years. I've come to enjoy her hugs though, almost look forward to them.

"She's going to be okay, Alex," Klara whispers against my chest, squeezing me a little tighter.

"I know." I pat her back, swallowing past the burn in my throat. I will not break down in front of all these people. Especially the three men I work with.

She pulls away, her pale blue eyes glittering up at me from under wet eyelashes. I can tell she knows that I'm barely keeping it together by the small smile pulling at her bow lips but she won't say anything. I suspect she knew how I felt about Jessika before I did... before I allowed myself to. Klara gives me another small, reassuring hug before moving over to where Braxton sits across from me, wedging herself between Braxton and Stefan.

The medical receptionist gives us all the stink eye before bowing her head and turning her focus back to the computer in front of her. It didn't escape my notice that as soon as Braxton and Stefan entered the waiting room, the patients that were sitting close to us moved over to the other section of the waiting room. Four angry looking men in dark suits, one of them covered in blood tends to do that, but ask me if I give a flying fuck. I'm grateful they moved because if someone even so much as looks at me funny right now, I could crush some heads.

Where the fuck is the doctor? And why the hell is this taking so long? I'm no expert but it didn't take nearly this long on the numerous occasions when Antonio had to dig bullets out of my chest and stitch me back up. My knee bounces when I glance up at the clock above Stefan's head and notice that it's only been about ten minutes since Braxton and crew showed up. I swear it felt like an hour or more.

Several more hours pass before I can't take it

anymore and start pacing the waiting room. If someone doesn't come out and give me any updates, I'm going in there and will go room to room to find her.

I'm on my third trip back across the room when a woman in blue scrubs and white coat pushes through the doors they took Jessika through.

"Are you Jessika Tomlinson's family?" she asks, looking between Braxton, Stefan, and Antonio.

"I'm her husband." The words leave my lips before I have time to think about them. "How is she? Where is she?" I lobby one question after another at her, and the more she doesn't answer the more my frustration levels up.

Finally, she raises a hand to stop my onslaught. "She'll be just fine. The bullet went clean through so we didn't have to go in and dig any pieces out. She's lucky, a few more inches over and it would've hit her spine. She's under heavy sedation so will probably be asleep for a few more hours but we're moving her now and you'll be able to see her soon."

"Thank you, doctor," Klara says when words fail me… again.

"A nurse will be out to collect you when she's settled in her room," the doctor says before nodding and leaving us standing in a group in the middle of the waiting room.

***

The nurse warned me not to freak out when I walked into Jessika's hospital room, but no amount of warning could've prepared me for what I saw. She was hooked up to an IV line as well as an oxygen tank, however, that's not what had my steps faltering, she looked so pale and so small. Not at all like my little spitfire. Not at all like the woman who rushed me with a combat knife, who took down four armed men – I may not have been there but I know without a doubt that she was the one responsible for the scene at the club earlier- I wanted her to open her eyes, to lash out at me again. I wanted to see those emerald eyes on fire – anger, passion, lust, love – it didn't matter I'd take it all.

I pulled a chair up as close as it'd get to the side of her bed and that's where I stayed, with her hand in mind, and willed her to wake up for me. I didn't move when a nurse came in to check her IV bag, or when another came in to check her vitals and her wound. I probably should've, but I didn't give a fuck, they could work around me. Yeah, I knew I was being an asshole but I wasn't leaving my woman's side, not even for the few seconds it took for them to do their job.

Braxton, Klara, Stefan, and Antonio left when a nurse came out to the waiting room to let us know we could come see her. They said they'd be back later tomorrow when Jessika was awake. That was okay with me, I wanted a few solid hours alone with her.

It's another two hours before I feel her stir, and then those bright, green eyes flicker open and land on me. A slow smile spread across her face, her fingers weakly squeezing mine, and if I didn't already know it, I would now. This woman is my heart and from here on out, I'll do whatever I can to protect it. Even if she fights me every step of the way. God, I hope she fights me.

"Hi, Angel."

"Is the bitch dead?" Her voice is low and rough from having just woken up but I heard it.

I laugh. "You did good, Angel." I wipe the grin off my face with memories of the events from just hours ago. "But if you go off on your own like that again I'll bend you over my knee and spank that round ass."

Her eyes flutter closed, a smile still plastered on her face. "Promises, promises," she says before the combination of sleep and meds claim her again.

This woman is going to send me to an early grave I can just see it now.

***

"I'll tell you this, if that bitch hadn't died I would've killed her myself," I say several days later when we're all gathered in Braxton's home office.

Jessika spent two days in the hospital. I was ready to bring her home after one but her doctor insisted that she stay the extra day for observation. I would've been more than happy to observe her in my house, in my bed, with my cock buried in her tight pussy. That's another thing I was told was off limits until she's had time to heal. I've had blue balls from hell since I've moved Jessika into my house after her release from the hospital. And if she keeps walking around the house in those skimpy sleep shorts that do nothing to hide her round ass, and those tight as hell tank tops, I might say fuck it to the doc's instructions of no sex.

Jessika wasn't very pleased when I told her that she was now living with me. She insisted that she could take care of herself but I wasn't having it. Which is why I *told* her instead of *asking* her. I already had Stefan move all her shit into my house while she was in the hospital and give her notice to her landlord. Okay, I admit I could've gone about it better but I wanted her in my house. It was going to happen sooner or later... my way just seemed like the fastest route for me to get what I want because I always get what I want.

"If I had known who she was I would've killed her years ago," Braxton says. He stares straight at me and I have a feeling I know what he's going to say before the words have a chance to leave his mouth. "I'm glad Jessika is okay, but I can't help but think that she got what she deserved."

Antonio sighs loudly, taking a step back like he knows what's about to happen next.

"What she deserves?" I seethe.

"She was sent to kill you, Alessandro, to try and take me down-"

He doesn't get to finish his sentence because I rush him, pinning him against the wall, my arm against his throat.

"Say that again, motherfucker."

"Alessandro," Antonio warns from behind me. "Don't be an idiot. Let the Don go."

The Don. Not Boss. Not Braxton, but the Don. It's a deliberate move, meant to get me to realize how much I just fucked up, but at this very minute, Braxton isn't the Don of the Famiglia. Right now, he's my best friend and I don't give a shit if attacking him the way I just did was wrong. Jessika might be a lot of things but she did not deserve to be used as a pawn in her father's game. But I do what Antonio says and let Braxton go because despite how much I want to drive my fist through his face, my girl needs me at home.

I turn to leave but not before saying, "would you still have the same opinion if it was Klara?"

Chapter 20

JESSIKA

I'VE JUST MADE Klara and I a cup of coffee and placed hers in front of her when I hear the beep from the alarm as the front door opens and closes. Alessandro appears in the kitchen a moment later. He's trying to look like everything is okay, but he's back a little more rigid than normal, his steps a little more measured, and I don't miss the way his fists clench at his sides.

"Alessandro, what happened?"

He's told me on multiple occasions that he'll never discuss Famiglia business with me, not just because it has nothing to do with me but because he doesn't want my safety jeopardized. I told him to go fuck himself. My safety was jeopardized the minute I was born to the boss of the Bratva. Organized crime was in my blood, I lived it… breathed it, bled for it my entire life. Hell, I began training as an assassin nine years ago on my thirteenth birthday, and once I reached eighteen when I wasn't carrying out orders from my father I was training. There was only ever one year in nine years where I wasn't working or training.

Alessandro eventually gave up trying to fight me and

agreed that he will share stuff with me… within reason. Obviously, he has no clue how powerful a woman's power of persuasion is because if he did he'd know that he has no chance in hell of keeping things from me, and even if he did, we're like bloodhounds when it comes to sniffing these things out.

Alessandro keeps glancing towards Klara so I'm guessing whatever happened, he doesn't want her to know.

"Oh, for fuck's sake," Klara huffs. "Spit it out, Alex. What did that fiancé of mine do now?"

I'm trying really hard to trample down the giggle that's wanting to burst free when I see how much Alessandro is struggling with what to do. You see, Klara has this way of putting all these macho men in their place. She doesn't give two fucks that they're the Italian Mafia, one of *the* most feared crime families on this side of the country. The woman has giant lady balls, I'll give her that. I get a sick pleasure in watching her make these men cower. Did I say that she's only five-three?

Finally, Alessandro relaxes his stance, leans back against the counter across from us and casually crosses his arms over his massive hulk chest. I have to clench my thighs and swallow a whimper when his biceps bulge under the cotton shirt. Secretly, I wish the short sleeves would tear apart under the pressure and he'd go pure Hulk by ripping the cotton material off his body. I fight back a groan, but when he smirks at me I know I didn't do a very good job at hiding it. It's been way too fucking long since I've had… well, a good fucking.

"Sorry baby girl," Alessandro says to Klara. "That tone and those puppy dog eyes aren't going to work this time. If you want to know what went down, you need to ask the boss."

Klara pouts, pushing out her bottom lip dramatically in what I'm guessing is hope that Alessandro will crumble and tell her, but he stands firm and doesn't give in to her shenanigans.

"Fine," she sighs, grabbing her purse from the back of the chair when she stands. "Jessika, I'll call you tomorrow and let you know what time Sofia says for coffee."

"Sounds good, K." I hug her and both Alessandro and I watch as she leaves without even so much as a goodbye to him.

When I look up at him, he looks a little hurt. If I wasn't secure in my knowledge about what Alessandro feels for me and in knowing that his relationship with Klara is strictly brotherly in nature then I would be slightly envious of how close they are and the hurt look on his face when Klara left without another word to him.

"Alright," I say, moving to stand in front of him. "What *did* go down today with Braxton?"

Alessandro releases a breath I didn't know he was holding and pulls me into his solid chest. "It's not something you need to worry about, Angel," he says placing a soft kiss on my forehead and I swoon. I've never had a guy kiss my forehead before but Alessandro did it one time and I was hooked. It is now one of my favorite things he does, the other being making me come like it's going out of style. And okay, the way he loves me is another favorite. I just wish he would tell me those three little words.

A smirk up at him all the while my fingers trail down the front of his chest to popping open the buttons on his jeans. One dark eyebrow raises in question, that doesn't stop me from getting to my knees, hooking my fingers into the waistband of the denim and pulling them down to his mid-thigh. Another thing I love about Alessandro, he goes commando about ninety percent of the time. Easy access. I grip his hardening length in my palm and lick from base to tip making sure to lick his slit.

Alessandro hisses, his hands flying to the back of my head but he doesn't pull my head down forcing me to take his full length, nor does he yank me off.

"Jess," he says between clenched teeth. "The doctor said no sex for several weeks." I can hear the whine in his voice. He wants this as much as I do but he's trying to be a gentleman and put my healing first.

"Baby, I'm injured, not dead. Plus, my mouth is just fine, thank you very much. And if I want to get my boyfriend off then I'm going to get him off. Is that a problem?"

Alessandro growls and I take that as my answer to continue. I flatten my tongue against his length and lick from base to tip, swirling my tongue around the head this time before wrapping my lips around his thick cock and taking him in as far as I can go. Alessandro's head falls back between his shoulders and his grip on my head tightens when I hollow out my cheeks, increasing the suction. His hips buck on a groan and I know he's not going to last much longer. Hell, I'm surprised he's kept his hands off me for this long. Well, no more. I'm not fragile, I'm not going to break, and I'm done being cockblocked by a doctor who obviously hasn't had the pleasure of being fuck by someone like Hulk. *My* Hulk.

Alessandro must see my lust for him clear in my eyes when I look up at him from my position on my knees because his grip tightens and then he's thrusting his hips, fucking my throat harder I almost gag around his cock then he's coming spurt after spurt of cum hits the back of my throat.

"Mmm." It comes out as a purr when I lick the excess cum off the head of his cock before licking my lips.

"Fuck, you're gorgeous," he praises me, cupping my face in his palm, his thumb running gently up and down my cheek. I lean into his touch, soaking in the warmth of his skin against mine.

***

"Okay," I say leaning back in one of the wicker chairs at our table at the cute little café just outside of town. "Spill." I look at Klara making sure she knows I'm talking to her.

She sighs, her shoulders deflating as she stirs her white mocha americano misto making sure the white mocha sauce has mixed with the espresso, water, and steamed milk. "What did Alessandro tell you after I left?"

I shrug, taking a sip of my coffee, looking from Sofia to her. "Nothing. He was kind of... er, distracted."

Sofia laughs and Klara snorts.

"I'm surprised the two of you made it as long as you did," Klara says.

I'm not even a little sorry that Alessandro and I can't keep our hands off each other.

The waitress brings us our lunch and when she leaves Sofia and I both look at Klara, waiting for her to continue speaking.

"Braxton apparently wasn't very happy that you're still in Alessandro's life. I guess he assumed that after finding out you're Amanda's sister, Alessandro would cut you lose. He... um, also said other stuff but I really don't want to repeat them."

It doesn't come as a surprise that's Braxton thought, hell, I've thought it a couple times too. I can also guess at what he said that Klara refuses to repeat. Braxton has never liked me, and I get it. I do. I was a threat to his family and that included Alessandro, but I would rather die than see any harm come to them from my doing. I killed my own sister because I knew she'd be the next one father sent, and I'll kill anyone else he sends. I even tried tracking him down after I got out of the hospital – to the dismay of Alessandro- but I couldn't find him. He wasn't at my childhood home nor at any of his known hiding spots. Which leads me to believe that after word got out about Amanda he tucked tail and ran. Whether that was to Russia or another country, I don't know, but I won't stop until I find him.

"It's okay, Klara," I tell her when her blue eyes grow sad. "Not everyone is going to like everyone."

She drops her club sandwich back on her plate and wipes her hands on a napkin before taking my hand in hers. "It's not okay, Jess. He was being an asshole. Braxton is a complicated one and I love him, but he's wrong about you. And I think he knows it too but he's too stubborn to admit when he's wrong." She levels her pales eyes on me and I squirm in my seat. "And he is wrong, Jessika."

Sofia nods along with everything Klara says. God, I love these women. Aside from Mel, I've never had female friends. My sister was certainly never a friend, nor did she try to be one. My heart tightens when I realize that I more than anything wish that these ladies, including Mel, were my sisters.

"Thanks, K."

"Alright, enough of this," she says, gripping Sofia's hand in her other one. "There was a reason I invited the two of you to coffee... or um, lunch now I guess." The three of us giggle.

Klara did say coffee when we set it up but by the time the three of us got to the café, we realized that none of us had eaten that morning and that lead to us ordering sandwiches to go along with our coffees.

Klara clears her throat, her eyes welling with tears and I briefly wonder if another felony will be in my very near future, but then she shocks me with what she says next. "Will you be my bridesmaids?"

I stare at her, open-mouthed, not entirely sure if I heard her correctly. Klara must take our silence for something else because she starts rambling which is the usual tell that she's nervous. "I mean, Adrienne already said yes to being my maid of honor, but if you want the job it's yours. I just can't see myself standing up at the altar of the biggest day of my life without the two of you..."

"Klara," I interrupt her torment by gently squeezing the hand that's in mine. "I'd be honored to be your bridesmaid, and I think Adrienne should be your maid of honor. She is your best friend after all."

"I agree," Sofia says. "Adrienne should be your maid of honor. I'm honored you'd want me as your bridesmaid... even though I'm just Braxton's cousin."

"Which makes you my cousin," Klara replies with a reassuring smile.

"When's the wedding?" I ask, curious because Alessandro hasn't mentioned anything about Braxton and Klara getting married. I mean I knew they were engaged but there was no wedding talk at the family dinner.

"Oh, um…" Klara looks down at the sandwich on her plate, a deep blush appearing on her cheeks. "It's um, kinda this weekend," she mumbles.

"That's funny, I thought you just said this weekend," Sofia lets out a nervous laugh.

"I… did," Klara says lifting her eyes to meet Sofia and I's shocked ones. "We have an appointment at the dress store after this. Adrienne is meeting us there."

Oh man, if she wasn't freaking gorgeous and my only way of convincing Braxton that I'm not a threat, I'd strangle her right now. Only in the most loving, sisterly way of course.

"Well," I start, gulping down the rest of my kind-of-cold-coffee, "guess we're going shopping," I grin at Klara and watch as she visibly relaxes before us.

Chapter 21

ALESSANDRO

I NEVER THOUGHT I'd be standing next to my best friend on the day of his wedding and watching the love of my love walk towards the altar in a long, black bridesmaid's dress that accentuates all her curves but still leaves a lot to the imagination, wishing it was a white one and this was our wedding. Hell, I never thought I'd ever fall in love. Let alone find someone who could match my fight with her own. Neither did Braxton with Klara.

We were certain that love should never play a part in our lives because it was a recipe for disaster. There was already too much bloodshed on a daily basis, we couldn't imagine if one day that blood happened to belong to those we loved. I prayed there was never a repeat of what happened to Jessika or Klara.

It didn't take him long to realize that Klara was what made his life worth living. It took me awhile to realize that I would rather spend every day of my life fighting with Jessika than live without her.

It took her awhile but she confided in me this past week the fact that her parents forced her to have a hysterectomy when she was younger. Which meant, she would never get pregnant. I wanted to hunt the fucker down and introduce him to a few of my tools, and a whole new world of hurt. I would've too if Jessika hadn't curled up into my side and sobbed. Her parents stole something from her that she'd never be able to get back. Yes, she could have kids through channels like adoption and a surrogate. But she'll never get to experience being pregnant. She'll never get to feel the baby kick from inside her, she'll never experience labor. None of it. It was all stolen from her. And for what? So that when the time came she would make the ultimate weapon.

They failed to realize that there was a part of Jessika they would never be able to take. Jessika wasn't like them. She couldn't turn off her feelings, and when she loved, she loved hard. Nothing and No one would and will ever come between her and the things or people she loves.

Her father may have escaped across the border after Jessika killed her sister, Amanda, but we would find him. Of that, I had no doubt. Jess had no idea that I was successful in tracking down her piece of shit father, and I wasn't about to tell her. I knew that she's been looking on her own time, but I want her to enjoy her newfound freedom for a little while longer before I confess to my findings. Truth be told, if I had my way, I'd send some of the soldiers to take care of him quietly and make it look like an accident, but I could never rob Jessika of that revenge.

The ceremony goes by in a blur. Gun to my head, I wouldn't be able to say what the pastor said or what was exchanged in the vows. I don't even remember handing Braxton the rings. What I do remember though, is the way Jessika's green eyes sparkled, the way her chin wobbled as she fought back tears for the happy couple, the way her body looked in that dress, and my plans for getting her out of said dress. I hoped to God she wasn't planning on staying at the reception long. I'll allow her dinner, cake, and one dance then I was claiming her for myself. Even if I had to throw her over my shoulder, caveman style, and carry her out of here.

***

JESSIKA

Klara and Braxton's wedding was beautiful. Their vows perfect. Klara never promised to obey Braxton, which I thought was just like her. She'd keep him on his toes for the rest of his life. I haven't known Braxton long, or very well, but I think she's just the type of person he needs in his life. Someone who'll love him unconditionally, faults and all... bossy assholeness and all too. I don't even care if that's not a word, it is now.

Dinner was delicious. Klara had said that Braxton's Ma insisted on taking care of all the food, and you do not get between an Italian mother and her cooking. I don't think I could eat another bite of seafood fettuccine even if I tried.

A voice clearing behind me as me snapping my head around. Braxton stands with his hands in the pockets of his pants, head bent. He looks like a kid who just got called into the principal's office.

"Jessika," he says, clearing his throat and looking around the room before allowing his gaze to travel back to me.

"Braxton."

"Look, I um, I realize that my actions and words

over the last several days may not have been warranted."

"Oookay," I draw out not entirely sure I know where he's going with this.

Braxton swallows hard before continuing. "I'm sorry."

Alright well, I wasn't expecting that. And while I accept his apology I can't help the giggle. "How much did that hurt?"

If I didn't know any better I'd think the Don of the Famiglia just rolled his eyes at me while adjusting the tie around his neck. "So much," he says with a smirk. "I mean it, Jessika. I am sorry. You are a part of this family now and Klara was right. Our family does protect its own. We'll help you end this thing with your father."

"Thank you, Braxton. I appreciate that."

Braxton doesn't know whether he should hug me, shake my hand or just walk away. I take pity on him and hold out my hand for a shake just as the beginning notes of a song dance through the speakers, and he goes in search of his new bride.

Their first dance as a married couple is to "At Last" by Etta James, which I think took everyone by surprise. I know I was expecting some rock ballad, but the song fits the two of them perfectly.

When the song started and Braxton pulled Klara close, Alessandro's eyes locked on mine and never wavered for the entire tune. But when Nat King Cole's "Unforgettable" started playing, he suddenly appeared at my side and pulled me to the dance floor behind him.

For the rest of my life, I'll never forget this feeling. This feeling of being held against him, his warm hand resting on my lower back, the other holding both our hands against his chest as we sway to the music. This feeling of being safe... of being loved. As the song continues, everyone else fades away. The newlyweds, the marquee, the people, all of it. It all fades until the only thing remaining is Alessandro and I and Nat King Cole crooning from the speakers.

When the song ends, Alessandro leads us away from the wedding reception, and down a small, grassy hill toward a little pond. His one hand is in the pocket of his black dress pants, the other grips my hand as we stare out over the small body of water. Alessandro releases a long breath, dropping my hand and turns to me, cupping my face in the palms of both his hands. His grey eyes bore into mine that I'm almost certain he can see down to my soul, that he knows what's in my heart.

"I should've said this long ago, Jessika. You're my heart, Angel, I don't want to waste another day where you're not mine. I love you and I know I haven't done a great job of it up til now but I promise I'll protect you with my life."

The dam holding my tears at bay all day breaks and I wrap my arms around his waist, pressing my head into his chest and inhaling his masculine scent. God, I love the way he smells.

"I love you too," I whisper into his chest. "All the pieces of you, even the broken ones you try to hide, and even the pieces that scare you."

Alessandro's lips crash down on mine in a claiming kiss and then he's throwing me over his shoulder, waving goodbye to our friends before storming off towards the hotel we booked for the night.

Epilogue

"**TO WHAT DO** I owe the pleasure of your visit?" he says, reclining back in the oversized leather chair in the corner of his home office. The fireplace blazing in front of him, sending streaks of red and orange across his face.

"Now, now, Nikolay. Is that any way to greet your only son?"

He scoffs, taking a drink of the liquid in his glass. "You are not my son."

"The DNA test begs to differ," I say, unbuttoning my suit jacket and taking up a seat in the leather chair beside him, a side table with a decanter and another glass the only thing that separates us.

"It's a piece of paper," he shrugs, crossing an ankle over a knee. "It means shit to me."

I pour myself a drink and recline back in my seat mimicking his posture. "And what if I told you I had the pleasure of meeting one of my dear sisters and her meat-head boyfriend. Does that mean shit to you?"

"Stay away from Jessika," he hisses, dropping his foot and leaning towards me. I smirk, finally having garnered his full attention.

"No can do, father. See, if I had known my sister

dearest had a," I pause, waving my hand in the air, "an adventurous side to her I may have made my presence known sooner."

Despite the dim lighting in the room, I watch as the blood drains from Nikolay's face but I keep going. "It wasn't my intention to go seeking her out right away but I followed her boyfriend to this club in the next town over and before I know it, he's inviting me into their bed."

"What do you want Kase?" His knuckles turn white with the pressure he's putting on the glass between his fingers.

I grin, taking in the dark walls and furnishings around the room. "This," I say gesturing around us. "All of it. I want it all, Nikolay, and as your only son and oldest out of your children, it stands to reason that everything you've built will be mine… in time."

"Over my dead body," he growls, and I chuckle.

"That is the plan, father. Over your dead body," I repeat and Nikolay visibly stills. "Oh, don't worry," I begin, placing my glass on the table between us, standing up buttoning my suit jacket as I do. "I'm not ready to kill you yet. You can still be very useful to me."

"This business will never be yours, Kase. I own the Bratva. They do whatever *I* say." He rushes to his feet when I turn my back on him like he did to my mother all those years ago. Choosing to ignore her and the role he played in getting an eighteen-year-old pregnant while he was married to his wife. He may be the head of the Bratva – for now- but I'll make him pay for every silent tear my mother cried at night when she thought I was asleep, for every meal we had to go without because Nikolay Romanov couldn't give two shits that my mother was working two jobs trying to support us, but it wasn't nearly enough. He's right, the Bratva do whatever he says but I've already put plans in place that will see an end to that and by the time I'm done, everything he owns will be mine. Starting with Jessika.

"For now, but what will they say when they find out you can't even control your own daughter? That the daughter you raised as a trained killer is no longer under your thumb?"

His steps falter and the expression on his face tells me exactly what I need to know. Nikolay has no intention of ever letting that fact become public knowledge within the Bratva because if anyone found out that he no longer controls the deadliest killer in the family all hell will break loose. Jessika may not know the true power she holds over her father so I'm making it my mission to enlighten her, and then... well, then I'll own her. Mind. Body. And soul. I've already had her body next step is her mind.

For now, I'll bide my time, planning my next move on how to get invited back into their bed. I'll gain their trust and then I'll do what Nikolay failed to do... get rid of the boyfriend, Alessandro. I could care less about Braxton De Luca and the Famiglia. I wanted Jessika. With her at my side as the head of the Bratva my sole mission in life will be complete. Is it sick to fantasize about my half-sister this way? Probably, but no one in this fucking family is normal. Plus, what my sister dearest doesn't know can't kill her.

THE END.

Bonus

BRAXTON

Four months later

"**K**LARA?" MY VOICE booms through the quiet house a few seconds before the door clicks closed behind me and I unholster one of the guns I'm always packing and lock it in a drawer in the kitchen.

She's not in the living room as I make my way through the house, unbuttoning my suit jacket and throwing it on the back of the leather sofa. It's been a long ass day. Alessandro and I had to pay another visit to someone who thinks they can get away with not paying back their loan. Fucker lost a few fingers and learned not to mess with me again.

I feel my shoulders deflate a little running one hand through my hair at the same time the other tugs at my tie just as my feet hit the tops of the stairs. My steps falter when I push open the door to our bedroom. Klara is laying on her back in the middle of the king size bed in nothing but a bra and panties. Her legs bent at the knee and spread out, her back arched, one hand palming her breast over the black material, and the other disappearing beneath her matching lace panties. The light from the white Christmas lights strung along the headboard illuminating her skin in a soft glow. Suddenly I'm very glad I didn't argue with her when she wanted to decorate our bedroom for the holidays. Unholstering the second gun, I place it on top the tall dresser by the door. Not being able to take my eyes off the scene in front of me, my tongue runs along my bottom lip. I'm suddenly feeling very hungry.

"Braxton…"

The sound of my name leaving her lips on a moan causes my already hard dick to twitch behind the zipper of my dress pants. Ever since Klara officially moved in I've been walking around with a constant hard-on. Especially when she walks around the house in nothing but my button up shirt with my scent marring her skin and her just fucked hair falling around her shoulders and down her back.

A low growl vibrates up my chest when I watch her fingers pick up their speed circling her clit. Her juices soaking through her panties. I'm on her in the next second, my dress shirt hanging open, hands pushing her legs further apart exposing her to my view.

"Ah," she moans when I lick her through the lace. Her hands fly to my head in an attempt to hold me where she wants me but I shake them off.

"Getting started without me, Mia Bella?"

Her breaths come in quick pants as I lick up her slit, sucking her clit between my lips before continuing to lick up her torso then her neck, nipping at her jaw, then pressing my lips to hers, my tongue demanding entry.

I feel the rest of the stress of the day melt away when her taste hits me. Rich espresso and caramel. My girl never can say no to those damn caramel filled candies and her coffee. Her two weaknesses besides my cock.

"And if you don't hurry up and fuck me, I'll be finishing without you too." She gazes up at me with hooded eyes, a playful smirk on her lips. Lips that were made to be wrapped around my dick... just not right now. I need her.

"Is that so?" I ask trailing fingers between the apex of her thighs and slipping under the flimsy fabric until I find the little nub.

"Fuck! Braxton, please," she pants.

"Please what?" I continue my slow torture on her clit.

"Please fuck me," she begs and I grin. I'll never get tired of hearing those words fall from her mouth.

Leaning back on my hunches, I grip her hips and flip her over onto her front, lifting her up by her shoulders until she's kneeling in front of me.

"Put your hands behind your back and keep them there."

She does as I command and I quickly grab the left-over string of pearls from the Christmas tree decorations from the plastic shopping bag in the far corner of the room. I make quick work of tying her hands with the pearls, groaning at the sight in front of me when I'm done. Fuck, she's beautiful. Placing a hand in the middle of her shoulders I push until she's bent over with her face pushed into the soft covers we recently picked out together like a fucking married couple, and admire her bent over for me, her panties soaked through and evidence of her arousal running down her inner thighs.

Curling my fingers into the fabric I pull, satisfied when it rips effectively removing any barrier between me and her sweet pussy. Klara groans when I press my tongue flat against her slit, her hips undulating when I suck the swollen nub between my lips. I can tell she's close by the little sounds she's making but I'll be damned if I let her come without being buried balls deep inside her.

I have my pants off and pushing into her a moment later. I try to give her a few seconds to get used to my size but she doesn't wait before she's rocking back onto me. I grip her hips in my hands, helping her slide up and down my length and watch as her ass bounces while her pussy greedily sucks me in.

"Brax…" she groans and I know neither one of us is going to last long.

Increasing my hold on her hips, effectively holding her in place, I piston my hips fucking her hard and fast. I know she can take it and I'm not disappointed.

"Shit. Fuck. Yes, don't stop. Please, don't stop," she begs, the walls of her pussy clenching around me.

Sliding my arm under her shoulders, I help her kneel, pulling her back into my front and releasing her hands from their binds. I need to feel her hands on me and she doesn't disappoint. As soon as her hands are free, she's gripping my thigh, her nails digging into the flesh, as I continue pounding into her and meeting me thrust for thrust. Wrapping a hand around her throat, I force her to look at me over her shoulder and claim her mouth again, swallowing her screams as she comes around my cock.

"Come for me, baby," she pants after she comes down from her high, my cock still pushing deep. "Fill me up, Braxton." She adds a little twist to her hips as she slams down at the same time I thrust up and that's enough to have me seeing stars as I pour into her.

Klara's head rolls back against my shoulder as another orgasm rushes through her.

Pulling out of her slowly, I go clean myself up in the attached ensuite bathroom. When I walk back into the bedroom to clean her up, Klara is laying on her belly, a sleepy, content smile on her face. My entire life I was led to believe that no one would ever love me because my life was not a life conducive to a wife or a family. But this woman with her curves, baby blue eyes, a stubbornness to be rivaled, and the way she calls me out on my shit has somehow managed to tame the monster inside me while at the same time kicking up my protective instincts. I lost her once before, I'd be a damn fool to her lose her a second time. She's stuck with me whether she realizes it or not. I'll protect her with my life. I'll make sure that every day she knows how much I love her, even if that means spending hours watching those ridiculous shows she's addicted to on Netflix.

I quickly clean her up and throw the washcloth in the clothes hamper before climbing into bed beside her and dragging her back until she's securely laying in my arms.

"Merry Christmas, Klara." Wrapping an arm around her, I place a kiss on her forehead, my heart swelling with the way she sighs a content sigh and burrows further into me.

My brows furrow when she pulls away a few minutes later, rolling over to her side of the bed. I hear the opening and closing of the drawer of her nightstand and then she's back snuggling into my side, handing me a piece of printer paper.

"What's this?"

"Flip it over." I feel her lips form a smile against my

chest.

My breath hitches and I think my heart stops beating for a second after I turn over the square of paper.

"Merry Christmas, Braxton."

I stare at the black and white image a little longer until I feel Klara start to squirm against me. Placing the paper on my nightstand, I roll on top of her, pinning her to the bed.

"I'm going to be a dad?" I ask, my voice hitching more than I'd like to admit.

A slow smile tugs at the corners of her lips, a tear sliding down her cheek. "You're going to be a dad," she whispers, her hands running up my biceps to my shoulders. "Is, um… are you…"

I slam my mouth down on hers, cutting off any doubt she has, but just in case she needs more confirmation I say, "I love you, Klara."

"And I love you, Brax."

"We're going to be a family," I say, leaning my forehead against hers. Pale blue eyes staring up at me.

"We're going to be a family," she repeats my words on a breath as I slide back into her slick heat.

Playlist

I Own You – Shinedown
Breaking Inside – Shinedown
Welcome To The Jungle – Guns 'n Roses
Moving in Slow Motion – The Sweet Remains
The Reason – Hoobastank
I have Questions – Camila Cabello
Consequences – Camila Cabello
Love Don't Live Here – Lady Antebellum
A Thousand Years – Christina Perri
Tin Man – Miranda Lambert
Woman Up – Meghan Trainor
All My Life – Foo Fighters
When You Break – Bear's Den
Raise Hell – Dorothy
Closer – Nine Inch Nails
Boomerang – Chelsea Williams
Say You Love Me – Jessie Ware
Million Reasons – Lady Gaga
At Last – Etta James
Unforgettable – Nat King Cole

Other Books by this author

Behind These Eyes series (can be read as standalones):
Skin Deep
Always You

Famiglia series (can be read as standalones but it is recommended to read them in order):
Dark Desire
Dark Betrayal

Standalones:
Coming Home – Appearing in the Me + You Summer Romance Anthology.

Coming Soon

Famiglia series:
Dark Redemption
Standalones:
Un·Breakable

Dark Redemption

Unedited sneak Peek

Chapter One
MASON

One Year Ago

The amber liquid burned on the way down, the ice clinking in the glass as I lowered my hand down to rest on the arm of the chair. The scene in front of me should have been enough to make me forget. To keep me in the here and now where all I had to do was watch and allow my body to take over while my mind shut down. I cursed as the two women finger-fucked each other on the bed in front of me even as my dick remained soft. My own body was betraying me. No matter how much bourbon I drank or how many women I brought back here with the intent of fucking, it was never the same. It would never be the same. No woman could ever measure up to *her*.

My wife.

The love of my life.

The woman I fell madly in love with at fifteen. The woman I couldn't wait to marry the minute we graduated. She was my world, with her long golden hair and bright green eyes. We had so many dreams after we got married way too young. Finish college. Go to law school. Start a family. Em had wanted to start trying for a baby as soon as I had that law degree in my hand but I started at the firm not too long after and begged her to wait two more years until I had time to establish myself more within the company. She agreed because she was always fucking putting my dreams ahead of her own. Two years turned into five which turned into ten. I saw the sadness and disappointment in her eyes but she never said anything because that's the kind of woman she was. I knew she still held out hope that one day I would come home and declare that we could start trying for the family I knew she dreamt about every night.

But fate was a cruel hearted bitch.

I had finally been given the promotion I had worked my ass off for. I bled for that firm and I was finally getting it. I had made partner. On my way home that night I stopped and picked up Em's favorite flowers and bottle of wine. That night was the night I was going to tell her that we could start the family she always wanted. Except when I got home, she wasn't in the kitchen preparing us dinner like she usually was. The lights downstairs were off which was unusual. She wasn't in the library I had built for her either. I did eventually find her... in our bedroom. Curled in a fetal position in the middle of the king-sized bed, mascara stained tears on her cheeks.

"Em? Baby, what's wrong? What happened?" My eyes quickly scanned her but nothing looked out of the ordinary. She didn't look hurt.

She never responded to my question, silent sobs continued to rack her body even as I curled around her.

My front to her back and pulled her back into me, trying to soothe her with reassuring words whispered into her ear.

It wasn't until hours later that I would come to learn the truth. My wife. My beautiful, intelligent, full-of-life wife, had stage four ovarian cancer. I was stunned. There was no way. The doctor had it wrong. It was a mistake. She was thirty-eight years old, surely they were mistaken. They had to be. I could not be losing my wife.

For the next few months, I dragged her to doctor after doctor seeking out different opinions. If one told me that she did indeed have cancer, I went to another and another and another. I forced her to sit through test after test, doctor after doctor telling us what she already had to hear countless times before. I was a bastard. An asshole to the highest standard, but I had refused to accept what was staring me right in the face. That my wife was dying.

Em agreed to chemo but after ending up in hospital again after the last treatment, her doctor admitted that her body hadn't responded well to the treatment. I, again, refused to accept that, but Em had turned to me with a small reassuring smile on her face, put her small hand on my arm and told me that it was going to be okay.

My wife, who lay dying in that hospital bed had comforted me when it should've been me comforting her.

It's been five years since she died, and I still see her everywhere. In the kitchen when I get home from a long day at the office. Sitting in her favourite chair in the corner of the library that looks out into the backyard. Her coffee mug still sits next to mine beside the coffee maker. The housekeeper still fills the glass vase in the center of the kitchen island with wild flowers… the same ones Em filled them with every Sunday morning after church, because I can't bring myself to tell her to stop. Her clothes still hang next to mine in the closet because boxing them up would mean that I would have to face reality. A reality that I don't… can't bring myself to face. It would mean that she is really gone. Em spent years getting this house the way she wanted it, and I couldn't bring myself to pack it all up. I knew I would eventually have to sell it. It was too much house for one person. But I needed to hold on to the feeling of her being close for a little longer. I needed to hold on to the scent of her as I step into our closet every morning a little longer.

I needed to hold onto *her* a little longer.

The one other thing I refused to do was allow another person to share the same bed I shared with Em. The hotel down the street from the firm suited my needs just fine. I would pick my conquests up at the bar located across the street and take them back to the room. The hotel staff knew enough to always have the room on permanent reservation, meaning it was always available for me whenever I needed it. Not sure why since I never stayed the night. If they fell asleep, I was never there to greet them good morning. If not, I made sure to let them know in no uncertain terms that I would not be seeing them again. I was not one of those dark, brooding, and broken men they thought they could fix and put back together. Broken? Yes. But beyond fixable.

After Emily died I used sex and alcohol as a way to forget. To numb the pain of losing the only person I've ever loved. The only person who ever loved *me* unconditionally. Sex served one function, and one function only. Well, two functions; to relieve my most basic urges and to make me forget.

And it had worked... until now. I could feel the tension is still coiled tight in my core and none of my usual vices were working.

"Get out," I murmured, gazing down at the swirling liquid in the glass between my fingers.

The moans coming from the bed instantly stopped. A few seconds later I heard the squeak of the bed as one or both women got up. I almost breathed a sigh of relief that they heard my near silent demand and left, but stilled as a small body straddled my thighs.

"Don't you want to taste her, baby?" The red head drawled. I gripped her wrist in my palm, haltering her movements before she could attempt to bring the fingers she just had buried deep in the brunette to my mouth. Any other night, I would've eagerly licked the juices from her fingers and bent her over the bed, curled her hair around my fist as she ate the brunette's pussy while I fucked her from behind. Any other night but tonight.

"Get. Out," I seethed, not caring that a little whimper passed her lips as my gripped tightened for a brief second before I shoved her arm away, causing her to stumble back off me and almost fall to the floor.

I've never once put my hand on a woman. In fact, I despise any man who puts his hands on a woman, but I don't recognize the person I am anymore. The red head mutters something about me being an asshole as the other one tries to soothe her and they gather their clothes. I don't bother trying to defend myself because she's right. I am an asshole.

If I hadn't been so hell bent on having the perfect

career first before giving Em the only thing she ever dreamt about then maybe she would still be here. If I even bothered to take the time and ask her what she wanted or how she wanted to go about seeking treatment for the cancer, then maybe she would've fought harder. If I had just been a better husband...

The list goes on and on, but none of it will bring her back to me.

"Fuck!" I roar over the sound of glass shattering against the far wall.

I don't stop to clean it up, knowing the staff will just add it to my bill, and grab my jacket from the back of the couch in the living room of the suite, the door slamming shut behind me as I make my way to the elevator.

I don't remember how I got home that night. Or even if I drove, which I suspect I didn't because I was soaked from head to toe. The only thing I remember is it was pouring down rain when I stepped out the lobby of the hotel and then suddenly I was in our bedroom stripping out of my wet clothes before collapsing on top of the comforter, not bothering to put on a pair of dry pajama pants.

I spent hours with my head turned to the side, staring out the double sliding doors that lead out to the backyard. Watching the way rain drops fell and ran down the glass. I was still watching the rain when the sun started rising and when the alarm clock by the bed went off, reminding me that I had yet another day of defending criminals to endure. My phone rang about an hour later and I suspected it was one of the other partners of the firm and my best friend calling it find out where the fuck I was.

I ignored it. All of it.

Chapter Two

"Jesus, Mace. What the fuck!"

I crane my neck slightly to see Corey, my best friend and business partner, standing in the door way to the bedroom. Somewhere in the fog that's clouded my brain, I remember I'm laying naked save for a pair of boxer-briefs in the middle of the big bed but I don't give a shit. Serves him right for showing up at my house uninvited and barging his way into our bedroom. *My bedroom*. God dammit, it stopped being Em and I's bedroom the day she died. The day she left me.

I groan and try to push myself up. My muscles protesting the change in position after being forced to stay in the same awkward position for most of the night. I hadn't even noticed that the heat never kicked on in the middle of the night as a shiver races down my back.

"The fuck do you want?" I grit out, sitting on the edge of the mattress, my eyes roaming the floor around the bed searching out the pair of pants I wore yesterday.

"You didn't show up at the office this morning. You're always the first one in in the mornings. Came to make sure you were still alive."

Something gets flung at me and it's not until my fingers wrap around the material and I unfold it do I realize that Corey must have opened the dresser drawer and pulled out a pair of pajama bottoms for me.

"Clean yourself up. I'll have coffee ready downstairs." He leaves no room for argument when he turns and shuts the bedroom door behind him. Moments later I hear him bound down the stairs then

194

his steps are faltering followed by a loud curse.

If my muscles weren't aching with every movement and I wasn't sporting a hangover from hell I would've chuckled at the likelihood that Corey almost tripped over Bowser. The big dog had made a habit of wedging himself right up against the bottom step and falling asleep. His dark fur blended in with the dark carpet on the stairs so you don't know he's there until you're almost on top of him or he shifts. Damn dog has gotten me good a night or two when I'd been so drunk I'd had to stumble up the stairs.

Five minutes later, I'm showered and dressed but not in my standard three-piece suit attire. I'd already decided that work could fuck off today. If any of my clients really needed me, I could take care of it from home, but I needed a day away from the hum drum of the office and criminals who counted on me to get them off the hook. I got paid the big bucks to look the other way and bend the law to my will to get them off scotch free.

Corey eyes my casual outfit but doesn't comment on it as he shoves a mug of steaming coffee at me and nods to the other side of the kitchen island with the bar stools. I heed his unspoken command and sit down. The smell of omelets cooking has my stomach growling, making me wonder when exactly was the last time I ate. If the massive hangover was any indication then it was at least twenty-four hours ago, maybe longer. Fuck if I know.

I expect Corey to start reaming my ass out for ditching out of work today once I've taken the first sip of coffee so I'm surprised when the next words out of his mouth are,

"How bad?"

"How bad what?"

He plates the first omelet, placing it in front of me before turning back to make a second. Once he has everything set up in the pan, he leans against the counter arms crossed over his chest. "How bad did it get this weekend, Mace?"

My headache intensifies and I'm not entirely sure if it's because of the copious amounts of alcohol I consumed over a two day period… on what I'm now pretty sure was an empty stomach, or if it's because of the force with which I'm clenching my jaw.

"It doesn't matter," I shrug, picking at the egg, ham, and cheese concoction on my plate.

Corey doesn't respond while he plates his own breakfast and maneuvers to sit beside me. If he wasn't my best friend I would've kicked him out long ago. Business partners be damned. But Corey picked me up in the months following Emily's death. During the first week I thought I had my shit together, thought I could hide my grief and bury myself in heaps of paperwork and cases, it quickly became apparent to me and everyone else that I wasn't coping with her death. That's when I started drinking, figured losing myself at the bottom of a bottle or two every day would help ease the pain and the guilt I felt around her death. It didn't. Corey found me at my worst, order a house cleaning service to clean my house while he cartered me back to his place and him and his wife, Melanie, took care of my sorry ass.

I didn't want to admit that my wife's death hit me harder than I thought. Real men weren't supposed to feel emotions. Isn't that the bullshit we're all fed as kids? Real men don't cry. Real men are tough. We're supposed to take it on the chin and move on. Well, fuck that. My wife died from cancer. The woman I've loved since we were thirteen-fucking-years old. What kind of man would I be if losing her didn't faze me? A cold-hearted monster, that's what. I lost the love of my life and I wasn't ready to move on without her yet.

It's not until we're both done eating and I've refilled our coffee mugs does he say, "Mace, you can't keep punishing yourself every year. She wouldn't've wanted to see you like this."

He's right of course. Em would've hated seeing me like this. Losing myself at the bottle or two of bourbon, using women in my own personal endeavor to forget. It doesn't make hearing it any less painful.

Without a word, I grab my coffee mug and bring it with me in a silent dismissal for Corey to see himself out, and head back upstairs but when I pass the open door to her library I physically can't pull myself away. Instead, I find myself walking into the bright room and sitting down in her favorite chair.

Hunched over with elbows braced on my knees and my head in my hands, I beg my wife to forgive me. I ask her to forgive me for not giving her what she wanted, for not fighting harder to find her the best doctors.

∞

Hours pass before I can't take the near constant growl from my stomach and make my way back downstairs. I heard Corey leave shortly after I turned my back on him and walked out of my kitchen, but not before I heard the telltale sign of the dishwasher starting up. The man couldn't stand a thing out of place which led to my making up a game shortly after we met for my personal enjoyment, and to see him nearly lose his mind trying to figure out what was different. Every time I went over to his house, I moved something. Just one thing and not necessarily move it so that it was obvious. Sometimes just an inch or two to the right or left, other times I'd just rotate it slightly. It drove Corey nuts, but hey if your best friend can't mess with you like that then who can.

Before I can sit down with my sandwich and another glass of bourbon, my computer pings with an incoming email from my office just down the hall. I'm usually not able to hear it unless I have my phone but I must have left the office door open and not shut down the computer after the last use.

Sitting down in the black leather chair, I curse as I see the email that just came in and who the sender is. So much for telling work to fuck off for the day because the sender of the email is not one you can tell to fuck off unless you have a death wish. Because when the De Luca family come calling, you better be ready to answer.